Does the Sun Rise over Dagenham?

Does the Sun Rise over Dagenham?

and Other Stories

New Writing from London

Foreword by Mark Lawson

FOURTH ESTATE • *London*

Contents

Foreword

Mark Lawson

THE PHRASE 'London fiction' brings to my mind a red double-decker bus being cut-up by a black taxi in a wideshot which also incorporates Nelson's Column and scattering pigeons. Or perhaps a longshot of the Houses of Parliament at dusk.

This is the London of film or television fiction, and not just those productions which are intended mainly for an American audience. The surface look of London has become a logo or trademark, a geographical equivalent of the big yellow M which means hamburgers or the curly white writing on red which means a fizzy caffeine drink.

It takes a big effort to resist this easy shorthand, to gamble that there is anything original left to show or say about one of the world's most famous geographical faces. It can be done. Hanif Kureishi opened up a previously unseen Asian London in the film *My Beautiful Laundrette* and the book *The Buddha of Suburbia*. Stephen Poliakoff – in the films *Close My Eyes* and *Hidden City* – also found new sights and sounds in white middle-class London.

But it's a risk. A critic might have lived for ten years in the suburb you have researched for two weeks. Better to try Glasgow or Idaho or Delhi or even Birmingham. Or alternatively, that other hidden city of the past.

The sheer familiarity of London – the unease that the writer feels in dealing with scenes which are part of the collective memory – is one of the three factors that has frightened many writers away from London as a subject in recent years.

The second is the cultural domination of America. Smartly market-minded modern writers have learned from their agents that an English setting reduces the likely size of the advance.

The third disincentive is political. A bias towards the English capital is now well-established as a political sin. BBC producers are urged to accumulate rail-miles around Britain in search of stories; letter writers from points north, east and west chide editors of what are supposed to be national newspapers for their focus on happenings in the English capital. Similarly, one guesses that a volume of short stories about London would be looked on more suspiciously in a Glasgow bookshop than, say, *New Scottish Voices* would be at Waterstone's in Hampstead. Regionality is a more fashionable concept in modern Britain than centrality.

These three pressures – the fear of cliché, the risk of penury, the possibility of parochialism – have meant that the capitals of fiction written in English in the 90s have become New York, Glasgow, Edinburgh and Dublin.

The two contemporary English novelists most associated with London are Peter Ackroyd and Martin Amis. Yet Ackroyd restricts himself largely to the past of the city in such novels as *Hawksmoor* and *Dan Lemo and the Limehouse Golem*. Amis – although he made Ladbroke Grove famous – has betrayed a commercial nervousness about the city, opting for Manhattan counterpoint (in *Money* and *The Information*) or an American narrator (in *London Fields*).

Modern London fiction, therefore, tended to come from slightly unexpected pens. Justin Cartwright, a South African, has brought an outsider's eye to two very commendable attempts at a *Bonfire of the Vanities* for WC1 and environs: *Look At It This Way* and *In Every Face I Meet*. And the crime writer Ruth Rendell has recently searched out areas of the *A–Z* which bear few fictional footprints: under her own name, in *The Keys to the Street*, set in and around Regent's Park and, writing as Barbara Vine, in *King Solomon's Carpet*, in which the London Underground system becomes the dominant character.

Perhaps the climate is changing. In 1996, a contemporary novel – *Last Orders* by Graham Swift – won the Booker Prize against a shortlist comprising titles more fashionably scattered in setting or time. The BBC's most successful drama series in 1997 were *This Life*, about London lawyers, and Tony Marchant's *Holding On*, a multi-stranded portrait of the capital now.

This volume is a contribution to the re-imagining of a city which many considered written out. Some commissioned stories from established writers Louis de Bernières, Nicola Barker and Emily Perkins are joined by the winners of a competition for new authors, organised by the London Arts Board. The judges were the novelist Rachel Cusk; John Hamson of the London Arts Board; Katie Owen of Fourth Estate; and myself.

The dominant style of the overall entry – though not, as it turned out, among the published selection – was what might be called Dirty Solipsism. This fashionable 90s style originated in writing which was allegedly fact: those broadsheet newspaper columns in which the journalist describes in weekly forensic detail – treating as unique the universal – the experience of a date, a taxi-ride, a dental check-up, a bowel movement. A parody of just such a column has recently become a bestselling novel (*Bridget Jones's Diary* by Helen Fielding) but too many young aspiring fiction writers seemed to be copying without comic intent those newspaper navel-gazers.

The winning entries reflected, we felt, a true range of London's looks, sounds and places, as well as a variety of writing styles and narrative techniques. With stories like these, London may yet come to be regarded – in terms of young fictional voices – as the Glasgow of the South.

Mark Lawson
London
September 1997

Hacivat

Damian Croft

MAŞALLAH! THE STRAINS of relentless arabesque and the smell of tobacco came drifting from the cab. The throb of the engine choked into silence.

Maşallah! Came the single points of orange light from the tips of their cigarettes.

Maşallah! Came the sounds of spoken Turkish that could just be heard in the hum of the London night.

Maşallah! Read the beads that dangled from the rear-view mirror.

Maşallah! Said the writing on the sun visor and the decoration on the engine cowl.

Maşallah! Echoed back the voices from the cab.

And then the night returned to grab the last two hours of sleep.

By the time Halil appeared next morning to unlock the grill over his shop window, an army of supermarket trolleys had gathered at the back of the trailer and children were giving rides to each other across the broken slabs of paving outside the *efendi's* shop. The lorry caused comment in the bus queue and turned the heads of people hurrying to work. Buses were pulling round it into the oncoming traffic and the stream of cars behind had almost been brought to a halt.

Selim slept on and no one seemed anxious to wake him. Mehmet appeared with a brush and began to sweep the pavement, then disappeared and returned a moment later with a bucket of water. The bus queue got shorter, the flow of customers to

3

Halil *efendi*'s shop increased and the children outside became expectant, then impatient and then expectant again.

It was ten o'clock before the door of Selim's cab swung open and a thin, swarthy man climbed out. He checked the strength of his legs on the ground beneath him and then crossed over to the shop and disappeared inside. He appeared again an hour later with Halil *efendi* and Mehmet at the entrance to the shop.

'Health to my truck! How many melons she carries! There is no truck in Turkey that travels so safely as her. How many miles from Istanbul to London and my arse is as sore as a leper's but my truck stays fresh as the rain! Health to my truck and health to the roads she has travelled!'

They walked over to the back of the trailer where the children had begun to amuse themselves with using their trolleys as ladders to scale Selim's truck. Talip, until now unwoken by these games, had slept on, stretched across the front seats of the cab. Now he appeared and came to join the others who were watching Selim unfasten the ropes on the tarpaulin.

Seeing the first slack of rope, two of the children snatched at a corner of the sheet and were rolling it back before Halil could restrain their excitement with a cuff. Talip struggled to deter another of them from cutting the ropes with a knife, but the truth was that everybody was eager to inspect the melons, watermelons that only a few days before had been growing on the narrow strip of land which surrounds the old city walls of Istanbul. So famous is this strip of fertile soil that everybody in Istanbul can tell a fruit that's grown there, and its fame for enormous vegetables is known through all of Turkey. And Halil was eager to test once more the reputation of the melons he had eaten as a boy.

Selim climbed on top of his load and threw one down to Halil who cut into it with a knife. Slice after slice he cut, drawing the eyes from the sockets of the children who grabbed greedily at them. Then, biting into the enormous grin-shaped slices they lapsed into satisfaction and for a short time the only sound above the noise of the traffic was the crunching of melon and the cutting of a knife. Then the spitting of pips; Tth! Tth! Tth! and the hands reached out once more.

Selim had rolled back the tarpaulin. Everyone knows how difficult it is to transport melons. How few drivers can carry their melons safely! Ah, but Selim's melons! Not one bruise anywhere! Not a single bruise you will find on Selim's lovely melons! What fine melons your old Selim can transport! *Maşallah!* Selim's melons travel well, Selim's the man to transport melons!

'Health to your hands!'

'These melons are as bright and as beautiful as Turkey!'

'And health to old Selim Bey, that Allah may grant him the life to bring us many more melons like these!'

Their praise was written in their dripping smiles and on the sticky fingers which they wiped on each others' backs. Selim had indeed brought them some fine melons. Quite the juiciest melons that had ever been tasted in London.

'Praise to Selim and praise to the fertile land beside the walls of old Istanbul!'

Halil had walked over to the store beside his shop and was unlocking it while the children began to gather around the trailer with cradled arms and waiting trolleys. Thwack! came the first melon, heavier than expected. Then Thwack! Thwack! as the children caught hold of the melons and began bundling them into the trolleys. Once filled they were pushed across the pavement into the store where Halil and Mehmet were already up to their knees in melons. Thwack! the melons kept coming and the sound of busy trolley wheels on the broken concrete whirred like flies through the heat of the summer morning.

Selim was keeping them busy, allowing no rest as he continued to hurl melons from the back of his truck to the children loading the trolleys. He began to sing. Turkish songs. Songs he knew so well from the videos he loved to spend money on. Beautiful Turkish music! The strumming of a *saz* which kept him from loneliness on those long Anatolian highways! Praise be to Allah for the *saz*! These melons were making him happy. How large they were and how beautifully firm. These were melons worth singing about. Not like the melons that would arrive on the boats from Italy. How could you sing about them?

Halil *efendi* was grinning too. Grinning at the space in his store slowly being taken by melons. This summer he would make money. This summer all the other shopkeepers on Green Lanes would be buying their melons from him and then everyone in the neighbourhood would be eating Halil *efendi*'s melons. Halil *efendi* would become known for his melons and everyone would agree they were the tastiest to be had. They would be flocking to the *efendi*'s shop and the *efendi* would sell them more of his lovely groceries. Halil *efendi* was going to make money this summer and the days when he could afford to retire to the shores of the Bosphorous were getting nearer with every melon. Every lovely melon. He raised one up and kissed it.

Trolley-wheels humming, the young boys dashed back and forth with their loads. The brighter Selim sang, the faster he threw them melons and the more the *efendi* grinned, the quicker the boys loaded their trolleys. They knew that Halil was pleased and they could see their rewards grow bigger with the size of the *efendi*'s grin.

Talip had sloped round to the front of the truck where he leaned against the bonnet, smoking. These children can't have seen such melons before, that is why they work so hard. Melons are a pleasure in themselves. But the rewards of carrying melons like these! Even Talip agreed that these were the finest watermelons he had ever set his eyes on.

Tth! Tth! Tth! Against the orange glow of a London night. And only the occasional car.

Tth! Tth! Tth! The sound of the spitting of pips and a truck emptied of melons. Swept clean of its load, with only a black tarpaulin left heaped in the back of the trailer.

Tth! Tth! Tth! The sound of the spitting of pips against the planking in Selim's truck. And the empty skin of a melon pushed out from under the tarpaulin. Toothmarks on an empty skin.

Tth! Tth! Tth! And the sound of bones coming back to life. Bones that were crushed by the weight of melons, and had travelled in a tangled mass. Every hole in the road from Asia to Europe had shaken this pile of bones. Bones that had rubbed together like sticks and smouldered away in pain.

But Allah has carried these bones to safety and Allah can work wonders in London. He who has lived off sand will live like a sultan in London. And he who has lived off nothing but watermelon in the five-day journey from Istanbul is likely to live like a prophet. Allah will see he survives. Allah is mending his bones right now, he can feel his life returning.

But so little sleep in the last five days, lying on a mattress of skins. Eating melon for days on end becomes like eating air: there's a dying to digest meat. And the bowels! The cursed bowels! The bowels and the bones. If only it wasn't for the bowels and the bones!

But Allah is returning the strength to this body. Soon it will be fit to live. The cool air of the London night is already taking effect. London, where the air is clean and the exhausts are fitted with filters! The London that takes only five days to reach from Istanbul, but it has taken five years to persuade Selim Bey to stash him away beneath a cargo of melons. London, where jobs can be found and everyone has work to awake to.

Still all that could be heard from the back of the truck was the sound of the spitting of pips, but around the edge of the tarpaulin the discarded skins of melons began to show, pushed out from under the sheet. The tarpaulin was changing its shape and even tried sitting upright for a while before it collapsed back into a corpse. Several times it did this, each time it managed a little longer but always it ended up sprawled in its original heap.

The smell of smoke from the kebab take-away had gone from the night air and the interval between buses had stretched to at least half an hour. This was the time of night! There was a cough from beneath the tarpaulin. The confident cough of a smoker. Then the tarpaulin swung upright and fell from the figure who with the same movement struck up a match and brought it to his face. A thick, black moustache, beautifully barbered, came into sight for an instant and then as the figure shook out the match, it vanished again, to leave just the thin orange point of light from the tip of his cigarette. A beautiful black moustache and eyes to match, Hacivat looked at the night lit up by the street lamps and blessed his good fortune.

Melons, lovely melons! Melons enough to hide a man. Nobody suspects a cargo of melons. How easy it is to hide beneath their weight! How he had cursed the melon harvest in Turkey. The days he spent breaking his back in the fields. But now, how thankful he was for the melons which had carried him safely to London. How easy it is for a man to get to London hidden in a cargo of melons. How stupid are all the other Turks who cannot think up such an obvious plan. Of course nobody would expect a man to be hidden in a lorry of melons!

Hacivat was sitting smoking in the back of Selim's truck, feeling his aching limbs.

It was two days later that the police turned up at Halil *efendi*'s and demanded to cut open some of the melons. Three days before, a young Turk in Manchester had been arrested on suspicion of illegal drug-trafficking. There were rumours that the police suspected a link.

'But oh! How stupid!' Halil *efendi* threw up his hands in horror. 'Aren't my melons the shiniest melons in London? Who would want to stash them with drugs? Don't you just get high on the smell, the sight, the taste, of old Halil's most beautiful melons? And Halil doesn't need to sell drugs to get rich: he's going to get rich selling melons!

'And what are they doing, searching my melons? Any such contraband that might have come with them would've been packed off oh! long ago – off to the towns in the Midlands!

'But fifty melons you come and cut open! Fifty of Halil *efendi*'s lovely melons! Fifty of my lovely melons! And what can I do with them afterwards? No one wants to buy watermelon examined by the police! Only Allah would know what terrible tools the police might use to cut open a watermelon!'

The whole storeroom, as big as a shop, with nothing in it but watermelon stacked from the floor to the ceiling and from wall to wall and from front to back they searched; cutting melons open at random.

'Aha! And what should they find? Nothing, of course! But

pips and the juice of the most juicy of juiciest watermelons! Didn't I just tell you so? And look how it runs down your wrists, making your forearm sticky and staining your official white police shirt pink! And look how it drops off your elbows!

'The juice of Halil *efendi*'s melons which drips from the elbows of constables! And not a single ounce of cocaine to bring fruit to your search. Aren't you just ashamed at the waste?'

But Halil *efendi*'s rage had put an idea up his sleeve. As fast as the inspector cut open the melons, Halil *efendi* was carrying them over to the front of the shop and handing them out free to passers-by.

'Come and taste slices of Halil's good nature! Slices of watermelon. Never again will you taste such beautiful melon!'

A gathering formed on the pavement as people came over to taste the melon and curiosity turned to a smacking of lips, the wiping of hands on sleeves and the sound of the spitting of pips.

'Praise to old Halil *efendi*! And health to his hands! For really these are the most delicious of melons.' And once again, Halil *efendi* was hearing his name sung in praises.

It was then that he conjured up the plan of bringing some crates of beer from the back of his shop and selling them off at cheapo prices to anyone who tasted his melons. He knew they would come back the following day and Halil *efendi* would once more gain their custom. Just from handing out melons.

And so the police, who had come to search for drugs, ended up causing a street party and the man they had wished to shame, they had made the happiest man in the neighbourhood.

Praise to Halil *efendi*! And a cheer for the police for starting a street party that went on all night! And no drugs either! And they hadn't even found the old trickster who had hidden in a lorry of melons and travelled to London all the way from Istanbul. Who at this very moment was sitting in the back of the shop, smoking.

The Free Hand

Nicola Barker

For Anne

'IF PEOPLE ALWAYS resemble their dogs,' Evie said thoughtfully, 'then the blind would all look like Labradors or Golden Retrievers. They'd have square jaws, soft mouths and skin like demerara sugar, which quite clearly isn't the case . . .'

'From up here Mrs Coley-Wilson looks like a Weimaraner,' Will observed, staring fixedly down at the road below. 'She's a strange purple-grey colour, don't you think? And she has an unnaturally high forehead.'

Evie liked Weimaraners but wasn't particularly fond of Mrs Coley-Wilson, so she didn't respond immediately. Eventually she said, 'I suppose she is quite a funny colour. It's probably just bad circulation. That does occasionally turn you mauve.'

Will was craning his neck at such an acute angle that Evie could see the vein which ran from behind his ear and along the side of his throat, bulging out like a wormcast or a slim, pale twist of barley sugar. She longed to lick it. They were both standing next to a large window on the third floor of their office building. They were colleagues. Colleagues, Evie told herself firmly, don't usually make a habit of repeatedly gumming each other's jugulars inside office hours.

'But the real issue,' Will continued, utterly unaware of the *frisson* his determined craning had generated, 'is that if you're blind you don't get to *choose* the breed of dog you end up sharing your life with. In general though, every decision an individual makes is an indirect reflection of their own ego. Their own vanity. It's no accident, in other words, that people often resemble their animals.'

13

'Do you own a pet?' Evie asked, quietly considering how beautifully Will's jacket was cut and finished. It was a plain tweedy-brown outside but had a bold pink silk lining nestled snugly within. Expensive. It reminded her of a lazy tabby cat, stretching out its dark paws in the sun and then yawning. A sudden flash of fleshy cheeks and throat and tongue, a salmon-coloured tunnel budding and blossoming before *click*, the crazy coral was eclipsed by white. By teeth. Then the pink was gone and the white was smothered by furry lips and the brown was back. The brown . . .

He was completely out of her class. Will. William? Evie still shopped at Miss Selfridge alongside girls almost half her age. But she knew where she was with a less expensive fabric. She liked her nylon and her fleece and her polyester. She understood synthetics. She was soft but modern and had no pretensions.

'I owned a salamander when I was a child,' Will answered coolly, 'but I'm afraid it all ended in tears. Problems with a faulty temperature gauge.'

'Reptiles are always difficult,' Evie said. 'My sister owned an iguana once. A male one. They bob their heads and then spit if they're angry, which I always found slightly off-putting. She really loved him, but after he'd matured he became very agitated whenever she menstruated. He could smell the blood. He'd throw himself off cupboards and work-surfaces. It was a wonder he didn't do himself a serious injury. The vet said the smell of blood made him want to mate. He was frustrated. In the end she gave him to a zoo in Peterborough. Not so much a zoo, really, more like a farm, but open to the public and with other iguanas and everything . . .'

Mrs Coley-Wilson had now disappeared from view. Will turned from the window and stared at Evie. There was a slight crease between his eyebrows, but it was hardly a frown. 'I live in Stoke Newington,' he said, 'near Clissold Park. Have you ever been there?'

Evie shook her head. 'Never. But I'd very much like to,' she said.

Will ignored her. 'They have a kind of pondy-stream,' he said, 'in the park, with lots of ducks on it. Black swans too,

with red beaks and curly tails. Gorgeous. But if you look closely, there are these curious little wooden ramps all the way
along the edge of the river bank, and if you look closer still,
there are clusters of turtles on each of the ramps. Terrapins.
There was a real vogue for them after the Mutant Ninja craze.
Irresponsible parents bought them at a few quid a piece for
their kids. But they grow too large. They carry salmonella.
They *bite*. Eventually the craze passed and everyone just
dumped them . . .'

The phone rang.

'That'll be reception,' Evie said, walking over to her desk.
'They must've seen Mrs Coley-Wilson coming.' She picked
up the receiver. 'Yes,' she muttered, then, after a short pause,
'I know. We'll be down directly. Try and keep calm.' She gently replaced the receiver back on to its cradle. 'That was
Amanda on the front desk,' she said, 'I can't help thinking
she's become a little too involved in this whole situation. She's
actually been saying that Mrs Coley-Wilson was mad for ages,
but no one bothered listening to her. I think she's still smarting.'

Will rolled his eyes at the idea of Amanda smarting but said
nothing.

'It was the advent of the hyphen,' Evie added, pulling on her
cardigan. 'That's when I thought things really got strange.'

Will had been fastening the buttons on his jacket. He
paused. 'So she wasn't always hyphenated?'

'By no means. She used to be plain Mrs Coley. In fact I
used to call her Holy-Coley.'

'To her face?' Will looked disapproving.

'Not at all. I didn't do it out loud or anything,' Evie cleared
her throat. 'Only in my head.'

'Okay,' Will braced himself, 'so we're both absolutely certain
of our approach? We need to be concerted.'

Evie seemed momentarily disconcerted but then quickly
gathered herself together. 'Yes. At least I *think* so.'

'We manoeuvre her into the hospitality suite and then we
calmly read her the riot act.'

'The thing is . . .' Evie faltered.

'What?'

'It's just that I've dealt with Mrs Coley-Wilson before and she can be a bit . . .'

Will frowned. 'Evie,' he said gently, but with the tiniest tab of saccharin tipped in for good measure, 'we've already discussed these issues at some length. That's why I'm here. I've been on a Man Management course. I'm properly trained to deal with all eventualities.'

'Yes,' Evie sighed, 'I would've gone on the course myself only I had my wisdom teeth out that week.'

As she spoke, Evie leaned across her desk, opened the top drawer and from deep inside it withdrew a half-eaten chicken drumstick.

'Do you think you'll be needing that?' Will asked, staring at the drumstick, somewhat perturbed.

'I think I may,' Evie said, smiling. 'If you don't mind.' She hid the offending item behind her back.

Will inhaled deeply, exhaled sharply, then headed for the door. Evie tried to do the same, but instead of exhaling produced a small, slightly apologetic burp. She stared at the back of Will's neck on their way downstairs, fervently hoping that he hadn't noticed.

The office building adhered to a strict No Dogs policy, except under extreme circumstances (into which category Mrs Coley-Wilson fitted with perfect adequacy). This might easily have been construed as rather inappropriate – if any thought had ever been applied to the matter – given the fact that the entire edifice had been built in silent homage to the manifold virtues of the canine species. The building was home to a charity whose main source of income was money collected for the provision of trained working dogs for the visually and aurally impaired.

Mrs Coley-Wilson was unaware of the building's policy on dogs. She was blind. Or as good as. She could not read the signs. To Mrs Coley-Wilson signs were just pointless lists of blurry words. They held no interest for her. When she visited the building, her main bone of contention was with the revolving doors in the entrance. These she found to be a palpable offence. The potential rights of her Labrador were among the least of her concerns as she battled with segmented compartments made out of pizza-cuts of glass and felt her fragile shoes stick to the cheesily-adhesive rubber matting underfoot.

Her dog was called Toby. Mrs Coley-Wilson had won his intense, nay, *undivided* loyalty and devotion very early on in their relationship, but she had subsequently worked quite diligently – in the three years since he'd first been put into her care – to render him virtually feral. This was some achievement, expecially with a Labrador. Labradors are naturally about as feral as a bag of mallow. They are soft and syrupy and chock-full of a crazy, silky geniality.

Toby, though, in tribute to the strength of Mrs Coley-Wilson's personality, would urinate liberally indoors, steal food whenever the opportunity arose and purposefully menace obliging strangers. He avoided traffic lights and zebra crossings, preferring the buzz of the hard shoulder and the railway embankment. If he sniffed a bitch on a lamp-post he would meander for miles in hot pursuit, even though he'd been neutered and should have known better. His soft mouth meant he could answer the phone, but if it rang and Mrs Coley-Wilson wasn't close at hand, he'd lift the receiver, growl, then place it back down again. This small act always left him feeling rogueish and powerful, like a loosely-muscled, weak-jawed pit bull.

On entering the building, Mrs Coley-Wilson and Toby did a quick circuit of the potted plants. Toby lifted his leg against a variegated fictus then sat down and scratched at his collar and his reins. Mrs Coley-Wilson looked sightlessly around her and then hollered savagely towards the reception desk, 'Turn the bloody air-conditioning down! I can't hear myself think.'

Amanda – small, diligent, beautifully manicured – was sitting behind the reception desk, clearly not happy at the prospect of once again welcoming Mrs Coley-Wilson into her ambit.

'I can't,' she said.

'What?' Mrs Coley-Wilson bellowed, although she'd heard Amanda perfectly well the first time.

'I can't turn down the air-conditioning,' Amanda said, keeping her voice at its normal level. 'The system is centrally controlled.'

'Centrally controlled? What's that?' Mrs Coley-Wilson yanked at Toby's lead. Toby staggered to his feet again.

'We have this same discussion every time you visit the building,' Amanda said quietly, 'I think you must know what I mean by now.'

'Rubbish. That's just rubbish,' Mrs Coley-Wilson observed tightly. 'How can we have this discussion every time I visit the building when half of my visits are during the winter months? You don't have the air-conditioning on in the winter months.'

'Oh yes we do,' Amanda said cheerfully.

'Stop lying.'

'I'm not lying. We have the heating on in the winter. It's virtually the same thing.'

'I may be blind, girl,' Mrs Coley-Wilson's voice took on a righteous twang, 'but I'm not stupid. And I'd thank you very much to remember that.'

'And I'd thank *you* very much,' Amanda said sweetly, 'to keep your voice down. This is a confined space. There's really no need to shout.'

'There's every need,' Mrs Coley-Wilson bellowed again, 'because it's impossible to hear what's going on in this godforsaken hole with the air-conditioning blasting out like it's on some kind of hurricane setting.'

Amanda said nothing.

'Did you say something?' Mrs Coley-Wilson asked.

Amanda still said nothing.

'I have been collecting for this charity,' Mrs Coley-Wilson observed loudly, 'since 1964.'

'Well, that's strange,' Amanda retorted, 'because the charity was only established in 1976.'

Mrs Coley-Wilson snapped to attention. 'Give me your name,' she said, 'I want your name. I want it now. I want it straight away.'

'I give you my name every time we meet,' Amanda muttered. 'You're fast on your way to wearing the damn thing out.'

While Amanda spoke, Mrs Coley-Wilson moved towards the sound of her voice. She came to a standstill in front of her desk. 'I shall tell Mr Wilson all about you,' she hissed furiously, 'then we'll really see what kind of a smart-arse you are.'

Amanda neatly extended her tongue at Mrs Coley-Wilson just as Will and Evie arrived on the scene, but on observing their arrival she quickly drew it in again.

'What was that?' Mrs Coley-Wilson yelled, as if Amanda had actually blown her a raspberry. 'What did you just say?'

'I just said,' Amanda tweeted sweetly, 'that I thought perhaps Mr Wilson's filming schedule might be rather too busy for him to give a hoot about me or my air-conditioning.'

'Mr Wilson is *very concerned* about air-conditioning.' Mrs Coley-Wilson shouted, slapping her palm down hard onto the top of the desk. 'Very concerned *indeed.*'

Will placed a restraining hand onto Evie's arm. 'Filming schedule?' he whispered. 'You didn't mention that her husband was a celebrity.'

'Oh,' Evie considered this for a second. 'It's a little complicated,' she whispered back, 'but she doesn't actually have a husband. She isn't really married. She just thinks she's married.'

Will didn't like this answer. It didn't satisfy him. 'How can you just think you're married?' he asked, crossly.

'Well, she *pretends* she's married, then. To Richard Wilson. He's an actor.'

Will scowled, 'I've never heard of him.'

Evie looked shocked. 'But he's very famous. He's in a comedy programme called *One Foot in the Grave*. He plays a moany old man. He has a catch-phrase. He always goes, "I don't *believe* it."'

Will was still scowling. 'You don't believe what?'

Evie smiled. 'That's the phrase. "I don't *believe* it."'

'I've never heard that before,' Will muttered, 'but it doesn't sound terribly funny to me.'

Mrs Coley-Wilson – the pressures of the air-conditioning aside – seemed to have detected the subterranean presence of Will and Evie in her general vicinity. Her head twisted around. Toby fixed his honey-eyes on them and growled a little.

'Mr Wilson,' Mrs Coley-Wilson reiterated, and at great volume, 'is *very concerned* about air-conditioning!'

Evie took this as her cue. She stepped forward. 'Mrs Coley-Wilson,' she said, and in all sincerity, 'welcome.'

Mrs Coley-Wilson was not impressed. 'Who are you?' she

asked, blinking rapidly and adjusting her headscarf (which depicted the geographic landscape of the Canary Isles in exquisite detail).

Evie smiled. 'I'm Evie,' she said, 'I think we've met on several previous occasions.'

'I'm not being funny,' Mrs Coley-Wilson observed grandly, 'but I have no recollection of ever having met you before.'

'And this is my colleague,' Evie continued, undaunted, 'he's called Will.'

'Will?' Mrs Coley-Wilson's cloudy eyes swivelled towards Evie's accomplice. 'Will?' she repeated imperiously.

'Hello.' Will nodded at Mrs Coley-Wilson.

'Would that be William?' Mrs Coley-Wilson enquired politely.

'No. Just Will.'

Mrs Coley-Wilson scowled. 'That's ridiculous. What were your parents thinking of?'

'If you'd like,' Will said, 'we could move into the hospitality suite. It's a more comfortable room just off to your left.'

'But I don't like,' Mrs Coley-Wilson opined with instantaneous zeal. 'I'm perfectly happy where I am, and so is Toby.'

Will scratched his head. Evie tapped him on the arm. He turned to look at her. She winked. She waved her chicken drumstick at him, then pointed at Toby. Toby had already noticed the drumstick and was clambering to his feet. Evie began walking slowly towards the hospitality suite, brandishing the drumstick. Toby followed, dragging Mrs Coley-Wilson wordlessly along behind him.

Once safely inside the suite, Will closed the door while Evie placed the chicken drumstick high up on a bookshelf. The room was large and pink with pastel blinds at the window and several low sofas scattered carelessly around like crusts for the ducks. 'There's a sofa right here, Mrs Coley-Wilson,' Will said, throwing himself on to it. 'Would you like to sit down?'

Mrs Coley-Wilson was standing facing the bookshelf. Toby was balancing on his hind legs and scrabbling at the shelves with his fore, but to no avail. The drumstick was well beyond his range. Mrs Coley-Wilson put out her hand and gently touched the pamphlets on the shelf in front of her.

'Pub food,' she announced suddenly, 'high in fat, low in protein. Treacherous. That's why I was born visually impaired. My mother was a barmaid.'

Evie was still standing. She opened her mouth to say something but Will put up his finger to silence her. 'I'm afraid it's exactly these kinds of comments that have led us to invite you here to see us today, Mrs Coley-Wilson,' he said boldly.

'Pork scratchings,' Mrs Coley-Wilson responded, 'and pickled onions. The ploughman's lunch . . .'

'You usually get cheese in a ploughman's,' Evie interjected, 'and that's high in both fat *and* protein.'

Mrs Coley-Wilson slowly turned her head in Evie's general direction. 'Stop embarrassing yourself,' she said, 'you don't know what you're talking about.'

Will frowned at Evie, as if he personally agreed with Mrs Coley-Wilson's analysis. Evie swallowed hard, wiped off the remaining grease from her fingers down on the legs of her trousers, then buttoned her lip.

'The point is,' Will continued, 'that we've had several, in fact more than several complaints from pub landlords about your unconventional collecting techniques, and even a few complaints about Moby here . . .'

'Toby,' Evie said.

'Toby,' Will corrected himself.

'Pub landlords,' Mrs Coley-Wilson informed the shelf of pamphlets, 'are invariably alcoholics and liars. It's an issue of self-control. They have none. If you choose to believe the testimony of vagabonds and drunkards then I'm afraid there's very little I can do about it.'

'That's as may be,' Will continued, 'but we actually have some rather distressing video footage of you pulling the hair of a member of the public, a woman, who neglected to give you a contribution while she was quietly having a drink with some friends at a pub in Holborn . . .'

'I don't care,' Mrs Coley-Wilson observed. 'In fact, I don't give a shit what videos you have.'

Evie bit her lip and looked over at Will anxiously. Will was somewhat concerned by Mrs Coley-Wilson swearing so freely this early on in their discussion.

'We also have conclusive evidence,' he nevertheless continued, keen to establish the full force of his case, 'that you have been posing as an official from the charity. One landlord said that you presented him with some kind of pass which listed you as a director . . .'

Quick as a cornered raccoon, Mrs Coley-Wilson spun around from the bookshelf, jerking Toby down from his back legs in the process. Toby grunted furiously. 'We both know what you want!' Mrs Coley-Wilson spat out. 'Don't think for one second you've fooled us, you devious little worm. We know very well what you're after . . .'

Will was taken slightly off his guard by Mrs Coley-Wilson's sudden burst of vindictive energy. Evie, however, seemed calmly confident of what was coming.

'You want Him, don't you?' Mrs Coley-Wilson asked imperiously. 'You want to get close to *Him*.'

Will cleared his throat. 'I'm afraid I'm not exactly sure who it is that you're referring to . . .'

'We are perfectly well aware,' Mrs Coley-Wilson continued regally, 'that you are only interested in us as a means of getting close to our husband, Mr Richard Wilson, the actor. We are not stupid.'

'I know you might think this is silly . . .' Evie began tentatively. Will glanced over at her dumbly, momentarily in freefall.

'What's silly?' Mrs Coley-Wilson asked, her interest temporarily engaged.

'Well, it's just that I always thought Mr Richard Wilson was a bachelor,' Evie paused, 'that's all. I mean I could be wrong . . .'

Will's eyes widened and his lips slackened a fraction. Mrs Coley-Wilson froze. Her purple face drained into a floury-white and then she turned, reached out her hands, grabbed hold of some of the pamphlets and began hurling them across the room, towards Will and towards Evie.

'No one calls my fucking husband a fucking homosexual!' she screamed. 'How dare you! How dare you! How dare you! How dare you!'

Will stood up. 'Evie,' he said, and curtly, 'outside. Now.'

They both walked towards the door. 'We'll be back in a moment, Mrs Coley-Wilson,' Will said, although Mrs Coley-Wilson was still tossing pamphlets and gave no indication of having heard him.

Amanda looked on silently from the plastic nest of her reception booth while Will took Evie to task. 'I have never,' he said, almost panting with amazement, 'never, seen anyone handle a sensitive situation with less tact. What on earth are you playing at?'

'It's just,' Evie said nervously, 'I've developed a kind of a technique, sort of an *approach* for dealing with Mrs Coley-Wilson. She doesn't respond very well to reason, so I decided . . .'

'Forget your techniques,' Will said quickly, 'I just want you to keep quiet. No more comments about protein. No more provocative little interjections about homosexuality. Just let me deal with things in my own way and on my own terms, all right?'

Evie nodded. She looked downcast. But once Will's back was turned she glanced over at Amanda and silently mouthed the words Provocative Little Interjections at her, following them up with a delighted grin. For a few seconds both women battled to repress their giggles.

Will inhaled deeply, exhaled sharply, then yanked open the door to the hospitality suite again. Mrs Coley-Wilson was calmly adjusting her stockings. She was now perched jauntily on the arm of the sofa and flashing a rather well-shaped knee in the process. Toby was scratching at the bookshelf, his reins clinking loosely behind him. The floor was awash with pamphlets. Will picked a roundabout route through them to find his way back to his old position on the sofa. Evie, once again, remained standing. This time, closer to the door.

Before Will had even managed to sit down properly, Mrs Coley-Wilson started in on him. 'What on earth were your parents thinking of?' she asked, 'calling you half a name?'

Will gave this question some thought. Evie saw his expression change as he silently negotiated an approach. She respected him for it.

'I think we're on good enough terms now for me to be able

to confide in you, Mrs Coley-Wilson,' he said kindly. 'I think we're both concerned enough about each other's dignity and well-being for me to be able to tell you – up front and without any caveats – that I admire you enormously for the large amount of time and energy you've invested in this particular charity. But there seems to be a problem in terms of approach. While it's good to be straightforward, it can sometimes prove a little frightening and intimidating if people – and by people I mean members of the public – feel overpowered by a person or by a situation.'

Mrs Coley-Wilson was smiling. Several of her front teeth were grey. 'Will,' she said cheerfully.

'Yes?'

'Will,' Mrs Coley-Wilson reiterated, 'you are a very stupid man and you are a very boring man.' She turned towards Evie. 'And you?' she asked imperiously. 'What about you? What do you have to say, Little Miss Dirty Mouth?'

'Nothing,' Evie said, without moving her lips.

'The point is . . .' Will continued.

'Bugger off,' Mrs Coley-Wilson said smartly, 'you dull little shit.'

'Mrs Coley-Wilson,' Will said, his voice taking on a firmer tone, 'sometimes in life we have to listen to things that we don't particularly enjoy hearing . . .'

'La la la la la!' Mrs Coley-Wilson sang. Evie bit her tongue and looked up at the ceiling. Toby, meanwhile, made his way over to where she stood and began sniffing at her legs. She looked down and gently prodded him away with her foot. He returned. He could smell the chicken fat on the fabric of her trousers. His nose was suprisingly invasive. Evie put out her hand to ward him off again and Toby responded by baring his teeth at her. Evie tried walking away but Toby followed her. In the end she grabbed hold of a bottle of pot-pourri-scented air-freshener and squirted it directly above his head. Toby did not appreciate the pungent scent of pot-pourri. He gave a small, gruff yap and then returned morosely to his Napoleonic campaign against the bookshelf.

'What I fail to understand,' Will said staunchly, once he was certain Mrs Coley-Wilson wouldn't start singing again, 'is why

it is that you don't seem to mind upsetting potential patrons of
this charity when by all indications you have benefited enormously from the work we sponsor here yourself.'

Mrs Coley-Wilson listened to Will's point very carefully
while chewing off a slightly broken fingernail. Before answering him she spat the severed piece of nail out on to the carpet.

'It's a war, Willy,' she said eventually, and chuckled. Will
grimaced.

Evie placed the air-freshener back down on to a small side
table while listening with some interest. 'Did you say a war?'
she asked, then her eyes turned nervously towards Will and
she quickly placed an apologetic hand over her mouth.

'A war, Mrs Coley-Wilson?' Will parroted, pointedly avoid-
ing Evie's gaze.

'Do you know,' Mrs Coley-Wilson asked righteously, 'how
many blind people actually benefit from guide dogs?'

'I imagine a very significant number,' Will answered, and
with – in his own mind – an equal measure of statistical right-
eousness.

'Nope. Only a very tiny percentage,' Mrs Coley-Wilson told
her two knees smugly, 'only a smidgeon. Only a teensy-weensy
number. Giving money to the blind . . .' she shrugged her
shoulders expansively, 'well, that's a *totally* different matter.
No one wants to give money to the blind. But a dog? Every
fucking body wants to give money to a dog. Every fucking
body.'

Will was genetically programmed not to enjoy listening to
bad PR. He tapped his foot impatiently.

'But the universal benefit of a campaign on the dangers of
peanuts to the unborn child,' Mrs Coley-Wilson expostulated
boldly, 'the risk a pregnant woman takes every time she chews
on a cashew . . .'

'I'm going to have to ask you,' Will said coolly, 'to return
your collecting boxes and your sticky labels to us immediately
and to refrain from collecting on our behalf for the forseeable
future.'

Mrs Coley-Wilson laced her fingers together and then
cracked her knuckles. 'No,' she said.

'I don't think you understand . . .' Will gurgled.

'No Willy, no Willy, no Willy, no!' Mrs Coley-Wilson said.

'If it comes down to it,' Will snapped, 'this charity is perfectly capable of taking out a restraining order to prohibit you from—'

'Bollocks!' Evie suddenly interjected, and with all the unexpected intensity of a small, female Mount Vesuvius.

Both Will and Mrs Coley-Wilson's heads snapped back in unison. 'So what's your bloody problem all of a sudden?' Mrs Coley-Wilson enquired, after a short pause.

'My problem is with stupid talk of restraining orders,' Evie pronounced calmly. 'I simply won't tolerate that kind of shit going down in this charity.'

Will – temporarily speechless – opened his mouth to say something.

'And you,' Evie said quickly, 'can keep your damn trap shut for once.'

Mrs Coley-Wilson folded her arms over her chest and growled. Toby's hackles rose.

'Actually, I didn't mean you, Mrs Coley-Wilson,' Evie said apologetically, 'I meant Willy here.'

Mrs Coley-Wilson harrumphed, but added nothing.

'From what you have been saying, Mrs Coley-Wilson,' Evie observed darkly, 'I think I'm right in thinking that you are in fact working not for us but against us.'

Mrs Coley-Wilson sighed piously, like butter wouldn't melt.

'And that,' Evie continued, 'is simply unacceptable.'

'I don't care,' Mrs Coley-Wilson said roundly, 'I simply do not care.'

'So fine, you have your bar food campaign to conduct,' Evie persisted, ignoring Mrs Coley-Wilson's apparent lack of concern, 'and while I'm willing to believe that it is an important campaign, at the end of the day it isn't *our* campaign. We are dog people. We are interested in dogs. That's our thing. That's our bag. That's our brief.'

'Fuck dogs,' Mrs Coley-Wilson muttered.

'Exactly.' Evie said.

'Exactly what?' Mrs Coley-Wilson asked.

'You hand in your collection boxes, you turn in your stickers and your false identity pass or I'm afraid we fuck Toby over.'

Evie spoke with deliberate slowness. 'In plain terms, Mrs Coley-Wilson, what I'm telling you is that either you leave us alone or Toby here is for the high jump.'

Mrs Coley-Wilson looked slightly surprised. 'High jump?' she said inquisitively. 'Be a little more specific.'

'How much more specific can I get?' Evie asked, her voice low as an oboe. 'You get out of my face, and you stay out of my face, or Toby here will be packing up his little lead and reins for a long stay in that great big doggie motel in the sky.'

Mrs Coley-Wilson nodded her head thoughtfully. Then she scratched her nose.

'I have killed dogs before,' Evie continued, her confidence expanding with every syllable, 'and I mean naughty dogs, ill-behaved dogs, dogs that gave our organisation a bad reputation. I've done it before and I'd do it again.'

'Evie!' Will interjected.

'You know *how* I do it?' she asked triumphantly.

Mrs Coley-Wilson shook her head. She was frowning but clearly interested.

'I snap them in half,' Evie chuckled, enacting this process physically in a rather gruesome mime, 'I take hold of their two front legs and I rip them apart. Hah! Sideways! Boom! I break their chest bones, I snap their backbones . . .'

'But that would take a great deal of brute strength,' Mrs Coley-Wilson ruminated softly.

'I *have* a great deal of brute strength,' Evie drooled, 'I'm Mad As A Fucking March Hare! I possess what they call the supernatural strength of the truly insane.'

After a decent interval Mrs Coley-Wilson's devious mind finally began logging objections. 'I shall tell people that you've threatened my dog,' she said suddenly, 'then we'll see how tough you are!'

'And you really think they'll believe you?' Evie whispered. 'Wake up and smell the daffodils, Mrs Coley-Wilson. I possess video footage of you in a bad yellow gaberdine raincoat, boldly ripping handfuls of hair from an innocent woman's scalp. You think people will be interested in the testimony of someone who indulges in those kinds of nasty playground shenanigans?'

'Okay . . .' Mrs Coley-Wilson seemed short of breath, a

curious mixture of enraged and enervated, 'okay . . . hang on a minute. Wait a minute. I have another ace up my sleeve . . .' For a moment she seemed to lose her bearings but then she suddenly regained her composure. 'I have . . .' she paused – this was clearly a significant moment – 'I and I alone have the private ear of Mr Richard Wilson at my disposal. So what if they don't believe me? They'll believe him! Everybody loves and respects Mr Richard Wilson. Everybody admires the great actor and personality, Mr Richard Wilson.'

Evie was silent for a while. Will stared at her, his eyes bulging like two over-worked brown biceps. Mrs Coley-Wilson was grinning and rubbing her palms on her knees.

Evie sighed. 'Well, I'm afraid that there you have me, Mrs Coley-Wilson,' she said softly, 'but then WHAT THE FUCK!' she bellowed, 'I'm a bloody player, woman! I thrive on high stakes. I live for danger. Mr Wilson's involvement is simply one calculated risk that I'm going to be forced to take.'

Mrs Coley-Wilson seemed very much impressed by this answer. 'And the stuff about . . .' she asked tentatively.

'What stuff?' Evie replied innocently.

'The . . .' Mrs Coley-Wilson took a deep breath, 'the homo-sexual . . .'

'Say that again, you ridiculous female, and I'll sue your damn nose off your silly face,' Evie clucked. Mrs Coley-Wilson seemed mollified. 'You have your campaign,' Evie continued gently, 'and I have mine. It's as simple as that. This is a parting of the ways. Now gather your things together and shift your scraggy arse the hell out of here.'

Mrs Coley-Wilson stood up. 'I'm telling Mr Wilson all about you,' she snarled, but there was a deliciously rotten eggy-flavour of defeat in her demeanour.

'Get that stinking cur out of my sight,' Evie gurgled, 'before I kick its mangy butt from here to eternity.'

Mrs Coley-Wilson called Toby to her side. He trotted over obligingly enough, by his own lax standards. She used him to direct her to the door. Once there, she had little difficulty in finding the handle and opening it. She vacated the hospitality suite, entered reception, trundled past Amanda on the main desk, paused – 'and you can fuck off too,' she growled, before heading resolutely towards the revolving doors.

Evie turned to Will. 'Good, huh?' she said, and reached for the chicken drumstick.

Will was massaging his temples with a shaky hand. 'So you've always made a hobby,' he asked quietly, 'of snapping Labradors in half?'

Evie chuckled. 'Nah!' she grinned, 'I'd poisoned the drumstick as a fall-back measure. I mean I can manage a Norfolk Terrier or a Pekinese with no trouble, but a bigger dog might easily get the better of me.'

'The thing is . . .' Will continued.

'No,' Evie said. 'The *real* thing is that if you'd actually intended to do as you threatened, to prosecute Mrs Coley-Wilson, the press would have had an absolute field day at our expense. That was a very bad move, if you don't mind me saying so. That was an *ill-considered approach*.'

'And your approach?' Will asked, 'What was that exactly?'

'I made a connection,' Evie said, kicking the pamphlets into a scruffy pile, 'between Mrs Coley-Wilson, the actor Richard Wilson and the dog.'

'A connection?'

'They're all horrible, or at least they pretend to be. I reasoned that Mrs Coley-Wilson must rather enjoy the experience of horribleness.'

'Horribleness . . .' Will mumbled.

'Shucks William,' Evie tweeked her own cheek, 'it was really nothing!'

She strolled through to reception, tossed the drumstick into the paper bin next to Amanda's desk and then set off back to her office. Will followed slowly behind her. In reception he paused and eyed the contents of Amanda's waste-paper basket somewhat apprehensively.

Amanda looked up at him. 'May I help you?'

'You know,' Will said, 'it's only just occurred to me that Evie is actually quite a strange woman.'

Amanda frowned. 'I noticed that,' she said sulkily, 'absolutely months ago. But nobody ever pays what I say the slightest bit of attention.'

'Really?'

She nodded.

Will unfastened a couple of the buttons on his jacket then inhaled deeply.

'I like your lining,' Amanda said, twinkling.

Will glanced up. 'My what?'

'Your lining. On your jacket.'

'Oh. My *lining*.'

He looked down at the pink silk glowing like glimmering papaya flesh under his fingers.

'You like my lining,' he repeated slowly, then headed for the stairs.

Does the Sun Rise over Dagenham?

Doina Cornell

SATURDAY IS YOUR day and your favourite song's playing on the radio to get you in the mood:

The winter sun rises over Dagenham
It's Saturday let's have some fun

Diz flings out her hand for a moment's thrashy guitar chord then admires the flexed muscles of her bare tattooed arm. A line of scars stretches from wrist to elbow. She leans on the window-sill and smokes a cigarette, looking out at the back gardens and allotments where people are bending over, digging at the earth. The sun tries to break through an October haze which lies over the houses, the rows and rows of houses. Here in Dagenham the houses go on forever.

'Diz, listen to this!'

Kiker's lying on the bed half-reading a music magazine. It says your favourite band, GRRL, is signing at lunch-time in the Mega Store in Oxford Street. They're going up the charts with their Dagenham song. Kiker looks in the mirror and tidies up the middle parting in her long blonde hair. She puts on mascara and fiddles with the ring that pierces her eyebrow. She's wearing her baby-blue strappy sandals with high heels, a satiny mini-skirt, tight jumper with a bra that pushes her breasts well up and yellow nail polish. She likes to look good.

'Diz, where've the others got to? I want to go out.'

Diz shrugs. She doesn't bother so much with her appearance; she always wears her leather trousers. Her brown hair is

33

short; she doesn't wear make-up. Her only ornament is a silver nose stud.

Kiker lies back and rifles through the pile of magazines she brought along with her that morning. She looks at one on computers. Kiker is clever. She wants to do A levels, study computing and make lots of money.

They were both born on the same day, a year apart, and met in secondary school when Diz was the oldest and Kiker the youngest in the class. Then Kiker didn't remember seeing her around for a year or so until she bumped into Diz outside the Heathway shops. Diz had grown up from a skinny kid into a tall, well-built young woman, though she didn't smile as much as Kiker remembered. They were best friends from then on but Diz never said what happened during that missing bit of her life. Kiker knew Diz went to see a counsellor sometimes but thought that was the social services pressing her to deal with her violence, first of all against herself (the scars up her arms) and then against others. She has a violent temper, inherited from her father. He's dead now.

Kiker never knew her parents. Her mother threw herself in the Thames near the Docks. Father unknown.

The radio's too loud to hear the doorbell but Diz's mum breaks off from coughing over her first fag of the day to yell from her bedroom, 'Desiree! Get the *door!*'

It's Pastie. She comes upstairs giggling. She's plaited her dark brown hair so the two little plaits stick stiffly out either side. She has a ring through her nose. She got her name because she lived in Cornwall until the age of ten, when her dad moved up country hoping for better work. Pastie had to fight like mad at first to get accepted in school. It was her fierceness Kiker and Diz liked. Now she'll do anything Diz tells her.

'Joo and Tat've gone to buy fags, we'll meet 'em up at the Heathway,' she says, grinning mischievously. She's kept her West Country drawl.

Diz's mum comes out of her room.

'Will you be back late?'

'Dunno.'

'Take care, love,' she says. She looks worried, though that's her usual look.

'Yeah, yeah.'

Joo and Tat are waiting on the corner of Church Elm Lane before the rise up to the Underground. You slap hands together in greeting, smoke, and chat about last night.

Joo's wearing a mini-skirt, a short top that reveals her pierced belly button, and trainers. She's pretty and not too bright, the most likely to fall for some heart-throb whose picture's in a teeny magazine.

Tat, who's a little chubbier than the rest, and bites her nails, wears a long red shirt over black ski pants. Her mother, who's from Barbados, has cancer.

'How's your mum?' asks Kiker.

'Okay. Watching telly with the kid.'

Tat has a one-year-old son, whose white father has run off like Tat's own father did years ago.

You were all born and raised in this area, except for Pastie. You call yourselves The Dags: it's tattooed on your left arms. None of you carry handbags, but two of you have knives in your jacket pockets.

You know that girl gangs don't arouse much suspicion yet, so you can get away with more while the police are picking up the boys. So far you've mostly kept out of sight. But you want to prove your toughness. Your heroines are those sexy film stars who use their brains to outwit aliens and government conspiracies and when that doesn't work, blast them away with big guns. Getting a guy at the end isn't the only thrill in life.

Diz is the oldest and keeps you under control. She never gets as drunk as you and doesn't touch drugs either – the rest of you'd try anything for a buzz. But she once beat up another girl, who'd a local reputation for being hard; the girl's face was so swollen she couldn't speak for two weeks.

Last night at the bus shelter you let those girls know not to push their luck. One was so shocked that Tat had to slap her face to get her to hand over the money. Pastie had threatened them with a hypodermic needle you said had Aids-infected blood in and Pastie was skinny enough to be Aids-convincing.

Some of your grandmothers fought Ford for equal pay. Now you'll fight anyone who challenges you.

Kiker fiddles with the straps of her blue sandals and tells the Dags about GRRL. You're keen to go up West anyway. The GRRL signing is just a bonus.

You walk up the Heathway to the tube, past the Saturday shoppers going in and out of the discount stores. This main street feels so poor and familiar. But up West is freedom and fantasy, glossy, up-to-date, relevant, heaving with life, with the future. It's cool and clean like shiny white marble; like the airy white spaces of the Plaza shopping centre. And even if you haven't enough, you're still surrounded by *money*, you can almost smell it rubbing off the fingers of every passer-by. While Dagenham drags its feet, like a dysfunctional village that doesn't realise a massive uncaring city swallowed it whole years and years ago.

This is Kiker's view. Diz likes Dagenham; it has its own independent spirit she recognises and respects. It's the straightforward East End. It has values, maybe old-fashioned, but at least not posing and shallow. It's unlikely Diz would ever go far away.

The other girls don't think about it all, they just accept things as they are.

Overground on the District Line: Becontree, Upney, Barking. You crack jokes and laugh so loudly everyone looks at you. You don't think much of those you call the 'shaggies' going to the Embankment for their Saturday demo against the latest Criminal Justice Bill with their badges and placards and slogans.

East Ham, Upton Park, Plaistow, West Ham – fat boys singing football songs, why's that slag staring? – the wasteland around Bow Creek to Bromley-by-Bow and Bow Road, underground to Mile End and across the platform for the red Central Line. Kiker likes that moment going under the ground when you leave behind all that reminds you of the dreary East and there's no scenery until you walk out into the West. The Central Line had to be red, more exciting than the dull worthy green of the District. Everything fits your expectations. Dagenham Heathway is nothing more than a pretend railway station; Tottenham Court Road with its tunnels and passages and multicoloured mosaics is new and bright and the gateway to the other world.

The GRRL's hit song is everywhere. The raspy voice of some busker follows you down the passageways and up the escalator:

> *London girls, you're scary*
> *You're so sexy and so arrogant*
> *Oh so naughty and intelligent.*

Pastie refuses to 'stand on the right' like the escalator signs say. It pleases her to be an obstruction. You Dags laugh and keep on laughing as you slip out three on one ticket and Pastie and Tat nip in behind other people. This station is a challenge as there are always staff watching the ticket barriers. Today there's a big crowd going out and you aren't noticed.

You come out on the west side of Tottenham Court Road and push through the people round the corner into Oxford Street. Pastie looks across the street at the space in front of Pizzaland. That used to be her patch during last year's runaway summer. Diz used to come visit her. Don't fuck up your life, she said. Finish school. Why bother? Pastie argued but in the end she came back home.

Now there's no one Pastie knows on that spot where she'd spent hours and even days, selling the *Big Issue* with her new friend Micky, chatting to friends who passed by. She got to know a lot of people and that concrete space was like her living-room. When she and Micky'd had enough they slept in a car park off Red Lion Square near the hot air vents.

Micky had disappeared, maybe gone back to Ireland. Pastie still had a poem he'd written her on the back of a Tesco's receipt.

She steps into the road to catch up with The Dags who are keen to get to the Mega Store as GRRL will be signing soon. You stop off first in McDonald's so Tat can get a chocolate milkshake. Diz begins to get a little pissed off and nearly loses her temper when some woman slams right into her when you come back out the door.

'Look where you're going, bitch.'

Kiker follows the others single file through the crowd. She feels the Street enfolding her with its noise of buses and taxis and voices, and the crowd on the narrow pavement is overwhelming. You can hardly put one foot in front of the other. You brush up against strange men, you smell women's perfume, you're excited. You feel the big anonymous rush of the city go to your head, you're surrounded by the crowds and not known at all. You love it. You love all the looks of men you don't know and never will, the fleeting glances that flick over you one after another without end. Young, fashionable men – not the pub men and pimply boys of your home.

The wide-open entrance to The Mega Store breathes out warmth and music and its light sucks you in like a helpless moth. It's as huge as a temple. But for once you don't try to steal anything. Diz isn't in the mood. The GRRLs arrive, there's a big crowd to see them. Pastie and Joo get autographs from lead singer La Di Dah. They sing their latest hit, 'Does the Sun Rise over Dagenham?':

> *London isn't Paris-in-yer-face*
> *Let me charm you-oo-oo*
> *London says like me or get lost*
> *It just ain't my problem.*

> *No more angst*
> *No more decay!*
> *London girls see the bright*
> *Side of every day!*

The Dags know that this song is specially for them.

Once past the congestion of the corner the pavement gets a bit wider and there's more room to move. Pastie walks in front as the littlest one followed by Diz and Kiker, then Joo and Tat. You've that confident spring in your step because of being together and going somewhere – not anywhere particular, just out and about in the city streets.

Tat and Kiker can't resist the smell coming from the sugared peanuts stall and buy two bags. You look at the shoe shop and a little way on stare at the people eating lunch in the Steak House until the eaters squirm uncomfortably in their booths.

'They look so fucking sad.'

There's plenty to try out, test and smell in the Body Shop until the security guard tells you off for making too much noise.

'Don't be a nuisance, girls,' he says firmly, but with a kindly smile.

You scowl. Except for Tat, who makes eyes at him and says, 'Ooh, black man you're so big you scare me!'

And you go out under the disapproving eyes of the shop assistants.

'That shop's for middle-class wankers,' says Pastie.

Kiker's more drawn to Dixon's a little further on, to stare at the computers in the window. She wishes desperately that she had one. She wants to go in and finger the keyboards and try out what software's on display but the others think that's boring.

'Dag, you'll be in there for ever!'

'I'll catch you up in the Plaza.'

When they've gone she misses them and doesn't stay long. The all-male staff look at her legs, pushed-up tits and face, but she's lost in her schoolgirl dreams of money, technology and power.

All down the Street you try on clothes, hats and shoes, perfumes and tester lipsticks. Each shop is more brightly-lit, more tempting than the last. The sun's come out and it's warm enough to sit outside on a bench near HMV. You eye up any girls your age who go by and conclude loudly 'Fat slags!' laughing at their lack of fashion sense. You revel in bitchiness and lechy comments about passing young men that as much intimidate as interest them. The young men up West should expect it, observes Kiker sharply, for they're all obsessed with how they look. They're tarts.

'Oh no,' says Joo. 'Some of them are sweet.' She's a wide-eyed baby-faced kleptomaniac. Little things find their way unpaid into her pockets. She comes out of Mothercare with nicked baby socks which sends you into peals of laughter. Except Diz, who only says: 'Slow down, Dag. You don't need all that stuff.'

But Joo gives the socks to Tat, for her little boy.

Beyond the Plaza the larger shops begin on both sides of the Street – C&A, Littlewoods, Next, M&S – and as you go down the north side towards Top Shop on the corner of Oxford Circus, Kiker feels like she's getting smaller, or is it the buildings are getting taller? Top Shop is your favourite, it's so big and full of people and racks of clothes, slinky little dresses that barely cover your bum and sequinned mini-skirts. All those lovely things you can't afford.

In one of the changing rooms Kiker coolly picks up someone else's shopping which has been forgotten for a moment and walks out. She meets up with the other Dags at the entrance where they're watching GRRL on the huge video display. She's acquired some ugly green dress, but a beautiful red pair of mules with thin straps across and chunky heels, her size.

'For the cause of beauty, no scruples!' Kiker says grandly, ditching the dress and sticking the shoes in a different plastic bag for camouflage.

'What crap you talk,' remarks Pastie.

'But lovely shoes!' cries Joo.

Diz almost smiles. 'Just don't get caught.'

Some stinky old woman is already fishing the dress out of the plastic rubbish bin, and crooning:

> *When she was Good*
> *She was very, very Good,*
> *And when she was Bad*
> *She was Horrid.*

If Diz had a song it might be that one. When she gets the money, she'll buy a decent pair of boots from Shellys.

You don't go beyond the Circus, at least not for the moment, but turn back to the Burger King to sit by the window and eat chips and throw them at each other. You wonder what to do next. Then Tat looks at her watch and says she has to go home because she can't leave her mother and baby alone all evening. Joo has got a stomach ache and decides to go back too. Diz can't persuade them to stay.

Joo and Tat go, though reluctantly. The mood's deflated.

'Joo's no Dag,' Pastie complains. 'She never does anything.'
'Yeah,' says Diz.

The three of you sit there slurping a drink and looking out at the street. Finally Diz counts up what money you've got.

'Less than a tenner. Not much good for an evening.'

You come up with a plan, helped by Pastie's knowledge of the streets. Just a little hit that won't harm anyone. You nick from big chain stores and rich people. They don't care about you, why should you give a shit for them?

The streets behind Oxford Street, Pastie knows, are pretty much empty, even when a block away south it's packed. There are narrow passageways, cobbled yards and deserted mews.

You decide to wait until it's dark, so you make a detour down through Soho. The Hari Krishna people go dancing past. Kiker loves the girlie cards stuck up in all the phone booths. Her favourite is: Have Some Fun Cum Spank My Bum.

A closed-up newspaper booth displays yesterday's headlines. Child Rapist – Five Years. 'Reckon I'd kill a man who raped me,' says Kiker.

'You don't know what the fuck you're talking about,' Diz snaps. 'You don't know what you'd do.' Kiker's surprised and gives Diz a questioning look. Diz doesn't return it.

You spot cute gay guys and badly dressed TVs and people who from the back you can't decide what sex they are, boys with long, thick shiny hair and girls with no hair and no bums.

'Someone said, you know,' mumbles Kiker through the rest of the sugared peanuts which she'd found in her pocket, 'in the future you won't be able to tell the sexes apart.'

'God I hope not!' squeaks Pastie. 'I mean, I like it straight: men men and girls girls.'

The Italian coffee bars of Soho remind Kiker how she once had a young Italian in Parsloes Park. She met him in the summer when she was working at the Asda checkout. He lived in a squat in Stoke Newington and only stopped to buy a pack of fags. He waited until she finished work, got her completely stoned and took her riding on his motorbike around the Dagenham Dock area enthusing about all the junk there; she thought him crazy but he'd furnished his whole flat from stuff found in the streets, even TVs and washing machines that worked.

She never saw him again but decided her secondary ambition in life would be to fuck as many nationalities as she could, and she knew London was the place to do it.

The Dags go down Shaftesbury Avenue as far as Piccadilly and buy £1-slices of pizza. There's the tail-end of the demonstration straggling past on its way to Hyde Park, accompanied by a few policemen. Someone hands out leaflets: Don't Be Fluffy! Protest Against The Criminal Justice Bill. Diz throws it in the bin.

'Excuse me,' says Pastie to the born-again Christian in Leicester Square. 'But shopping is *our* morality.' Her two little plaits stick out either side of her head and she's got a devilish grin.

'You'll go to hell,' he says.

'Pastie, stop hassling the poor bastard.'

'Diz, *he* asked *me*.'

Back on Oxford Street there's still the crowds though night is coming. Pastie suggests a good place for their plan is around the posh Berners Hotel, she used to beg in that area sometimes. Before she met Micky, she lived just by there, on the corner of a narrow passage opposite a pub, in a person-sized cardboard box which she'd wedged on a ledge by the windows of an unoccupied office.

You stalk a woman from a NatWest cashpoint up Berners Street but miss the chance as she goes into a building. It's getting foggy. You can't see the top of the Telecom Tower any more, which is rising in front of you. Here's another, a man. He leaves the hotel and walks to his new Ford Mondeo parked in East Castle Street. You confront him at the entrance to Berners Place.

Pastie spits dramatically, looking at the man. He begins to smile in disdain, notices Kiker with a flicker of lust, but a half-second behind is Diz and something in her face momentarily unsettles him. Plus the shiny hint of a blade. This man knows about the streets, you can see he quickly understood what you're about before you even said anything. This puts you off for a moment and he stops taking you seriously. Diz comes up to him really close and looks him in the face.

'I know you,' she says slowly, so cold it makes Kiker shiver.

'Someone else,' says the man. He wears several gold rings and a shiny grey suit. He smells to Kiker of expensive after-shave. But what's got into Diz? You've only seen her violent in anger but now there's a powerful cold-bloodedness about her and Kiker's heart beats faster.

The man smiles again. He's tall and good-looking. He has white teeth. Maybe the tan's fake. His nonchalance is getting irritating. Pastie can't keep still. She's dying for trouble.

Diz puts the knife-point to his throat. 'Walk, mate. You know I'll use it.'

Kiker and Pastie close in and at last he's lost his smile. You force him back step by step into Berners Place. He's yours now. You can see his eyes focusing now on you, now on the street behind for some passer-by. But Pastie chose this street well. No one passes.

Diz turns the man around and walks him down to the dead-end of the Place. There's a girl to the left with an empty hypo-dermic and a girl to the right with the second knife. You know he won't try anything stupid now. You haven't just taken his money and run and he's worried. Kiker doesn't have a clue who he is but Diz knows and Kiker senses something big is coming. The man sweats. Pastie doesn't care if he's known or unknown, she just follows Diz.

'Stop here,' commands Diz. 'Turn around.' She's maybe twenty years younger than the man but he is obedient. Kiker begins to wonder now if he's actually getting a kick out of his fear. She begins to hate him.

'Dag, go watch the street,' Diz tells Pastie.

She has forced the man right up to the emergency exit of the Jazz Club. Kiker can hardly bear the strong smell of piss that has accumulated there. Music thumps faintly deep inside the building. You're surrounded by the rubbish people have thrown out of back doors. Steps lead down somewhere you can't see, metal fire ladders climb up past grimy windows and blank walls. These are the unwiped arses of buildings with shiny welcoming fronts on the other side, on Oxford Street.

'Remember Desiree, you pervert?' hisses Diz. The man

looks blank. 'Remember me?' He has no intention of remembering.

'He's enjoying this,' says Kiker. The man smiles faintly.

'Is he?' Diz realises something. 'D'you like my friend?'

He's confused but curious and nods slightly.

'She'll suck you.'

What's Diz's game? Kiker knows she's a Dag and must do what's necessary. Does Diz want you to bite it off? The man is so fucking *nonchalant*! He unzips his fly.

'I'll pay you girls . . .' he starts to say.

Diz pushes Kiker aside. She's quick. She always keeps her knife very sharp. The blood shoots up two, three feet in the air, but Diz steps back so no more than a few drops hit her. As if she'd expected it. The man drops to the floor. Diz stands over him.

'You don't know me do you? Well, it's five years on.'

His words come out incoherent.

'No, Diz . . .' Kiker can't breathe. She doesn't pity him but even so the sight is sickening. He's already unconscious. The blood bubbles.

Diz takes his fat wallet but can't find his car keys.

'Dag!' she gives a low cry.

Pastie comes running from the entrance to the Place and gasps to see all the blood. You must help Diz drag him to the green wheelie bin for glass recycling that's behind the hotel, its lid gaping open, next to black plastic rubbish sacks big enough to hold two people. You drag him face down holding him by his arms and legs. He's heavy. There's a trail of blood all the way but it's not so visible against the dark asphalt. He crashes down on to the empty bottles. No one has seen you. But now you must run!

You come out of the Place and go right into Newman Street towards Oxford Street but the sound of sirens comes from there so you run back and off west, Pastie leading. Take the back streets. Then you'll turn into Oxford Street and get to Oxford Circus tube station. Kiker curses her stupid high-heeled sandals. Maybe you shouldn't run but the adrenalin makes you do it. You feel such a buzz! Now sirens seem to be everywhere, and a police helicopter is cruising overhead with a searchlight. At the bottom of Berners Street you see mounted police galloping east down Oxford Street.

'What the fuck . . .' Diz stops. 'Keep cool. Don't run.' For the first time there's a shakiness in her voice.

A few people run past you down East Castle Street. A girl follows, running but not so fast. She almost bangs into you.

'It's May,' cries Kiker, trying not to laugh hysterically.

'Hey!' May grins, her face half-hidden by short dreadlocks. 'What's happening?'

'It's a riot! They just chased us out of Park Lane all the way up here. This street'll be full of riot police any minute!'

'Oh fuck.'

'Done something wrong?' She eyes Kiker's shopping bag. 'Bit of nicking?'

'Yeah,' says Diz.

'Come with me but quick. My brother's flat's just up here . . .' She runs north up Wells Street and you follow. Pastie glances left into Marylebone Passage and sees there's still a cardboard box there just as she left it, someone else must be living there now. She feels a million miles away from that innocent summer.

You get to the front door of one of the yellow brick buildings a young man runs around the corner of Mortimer Street followed by a police van which comes to an abrupt halt. A bunch of policemen dressed in riot gear tumble out and pin him down.

May looks at the intercom buzzer. 'Fuck, I can't remember the number. There's no fucking *names*.'

The group of police form into a black squad with their plastic shields and batons ready and turn into the street.

'Hey!' whispers Kiker, thinking at last. 'Look like party girls.'

'How can I!' May tugs at her dreads. She's wearing scuffed ex-army boots. Kiker pulls out her new pair of red high heels. In two seconds the boots are off and in the bag, and May's got red lips thanks to Kiker's lipstick. The police march up to them. The leader turns his helmeted head their way.

'Live here?' he growls.

'No, yes, my brother does,' says May in a silly voice, wavering on her heels. The men look you girls up and down and continue towards Oxford Street. Above you, a first-floor window is open and music drifts out.

> *The winter sun rises over Dagenham*
> *But sets wherever it pleases.*

The head of a young man looks out of the window.

'Hi, Steve!' yells May. 'It's me. Let us in!' The door buzzes and you push it open. May breathes a sigh of relief and leans against the inside of the front door. 'That boy they got was smashing shop windows earlier . . . like I was. We only did a few at the posh end by Bond Street. They're working on the pavements so there was lots of ammo. Man, I've never got down Oxford Street so fast! And meeting you as well, that's good.'

'It's two years,' says Kiker drily. At least May hasn't noticed anything. 'Where've you been?'

'Living in an anti-road camp with my boyfriend. We got separated just now. He'll turn up. Let's go upstairs!'

May always had a thing about cars. She was conceived in a Ford Escort. At school she called herself a car terrorist but never got caught. She did the damage uptown, on expensive vehicles – like snapping off radio aerials, Mercedes signs and scratching CARS KILL on the paintwork. Her younger brother Andy died in a crash aged eleven as a joy-riding passenger on the A13.

Her elder brother Steve's having a party. He and his friends haven't a clue what's going on outside. Most of them work in Soho for media companies. People are crowded into the tiny orange living-room. May greets those she knows but you Dags feel suddenly out of place.

May starts excitedly telling what happened. 'It was the end of the demo. There was a rally in Hyde Park. Most people went home but some stayed and wouldn't move from Park Lane. The police got kitted up and kept on charging us, but there was a park fence between us so it was pointless. Then they came round the back through the park and blocked off the Underground exits so we had to break out down Oxford

Street. They cocked-up – coz they've lost us now.'

Pastie listens with interest. Kiker sees Diz is looking pale.

'Where's your loo?' Kiker asks Steve whom she remembers vaguely. Didn't she have a crush on him once? She pulls Diz in with her and locks the door. Diz begins to shake and then sticks her head down and pukes into the toilet bowl.

'God, Diz . . .'

Diz drinks from the tap and sits on the floor wiping her mouth. For the first time she looks like a kid. She is a kid.

'You knew him . . .'

'Yeah.'

'Why'd you do it, Diz? Why?' Kiker wants to scream. 'You're completely fucked up, Diz, and now I'm fucked up too. I don't know if I don't hate your fucking guts for getting me into such fucking trouble for the rest of my life.'

Diz doesn't answer because she's counting how much money is in the man's wallet. Kiker sees the bright pinky-red fifty-pound notes. How many? Silently Diz shows what else is in there, a sheaf of photos of little girls. 'Two thousand quid, Kiker!' she says. 'That's your computer. I don't want his filthy money.'

May bangs on the door. 'Come on! We're on the news!'

Kiker redoes her smudged mascara before going out. One of Steve's friends is waiting to go in. He spots blood stains on Diz's shirt. 'Are you all right?' He has a foreign accent.

'Oh yeah, sorry. It's my period. I was a bit careless.'

He turns red and runs into the loo.

'Leave him alone, he's cute,' says Kiker, hitching up her tights.

May's boyfriend arrives. He says the police are cruising around arresting anyone who looks like a rioter. That meant they'd got a few trendy types who dress hard but never did anything political in their lives.

Pastie and Diz sit on the sofa with Steve's girlfriend Sam and smoke a joint. Diz makes an exception for once to her no-drug rule. She needs something to calm down. Her hands are shaking.

Kiker talks to a bloke who's organising Get A Life! seminars, only ten pounds a go, at Cyber Cafés throughout the city. She tells him she thinks cyberspace is a load of hype. He thinks her East End accent's cool. Then she talks to that nice Russian who got embarrassed by Diz. He guesses she's ten years older, and she wonders if she'll be able to knock off another nation tonight. She's got her condoms in her pocket.

Outside the open window the police and ambulance sirens, near and far, wail like they do most West End Saturday nights. And the CD plays on:

The winter sun rises over Dagenham
It's Saturday let's have some fun . . .

Mask

Dorothy Reinders

TALKING ABOUT THE downside of London – the traffic fumes, the car emissions, she said she might just up and leave, go somewhere else. She meant it too, she had asthma. But where would she go? Where else could she live? It wasn't a serious question. The absurdity of it caused a few weary sighs, like don't waste my time.

As we were talking about the downside, the upside came up. You could re-invent yourself if you felt the need.

If you felt the need. The way she said it, with almost the implication that there had been an element of danger in her life with dad. Now her association with him was over, she was probably nostalgic for a little of the old flash of casinos and clubs. I always imagined he'd trafficked in drugs besides, but in the version I heard, he'd left for Spain with another woman, not to get *away* from anybody, well, except from her. Oh, charming.

Her ex and my husband were father and son. And like father like son, wouldn't I be in the same boat as her one day? If things kept going on as they were, I would. And if she did re-invent herself, I would be interested in seeing the outcome.

I was the one most like her. I was married to her son but I could have been her daughter. Same pasty skin, dark hair, and a long-waisted *chanteuse* look about us both. In fact we were both singers initially, and we both continued to put on too much make-up, as if we were about to go out there and begin a set. I would see her putting on her concealer and blusher and starting with lipliner like a professional and for what? To go to the Ridley Road Market and buy cabbages. It was like gazing into a crystal ball and seeing myself twenty-five years on. So, it was with some interest that I watched her putting on this new mask of hers.

She wasn't wearing it when she came through the door, with her arms wrapped around parcels. The kids had seen her on the road, and they wanted her to put it on again. They think their nan is a card. She said she would, later, after she'd had a cup of tea.

So, here we are in my lounge, with her in the centre checking in the mirror at the back of the cocktail cabinet, between the red crystal wine glasses from the former Czechoslovakia.

Sitting on the arm of the sofa above me, one hip nudging my shoulder, as if for support. I can see all of us looking at her through and around the wine glasses.

She gets it into place.

What's that all about? I hear Paul, who shouldn't have to ask, ask.

Your mum's asthmatic, remember? I say, and read off the packaging: protects against diesel smoke, lead, tar, pollen dust. You see it's not just car emissions. Retains dust particles down to zero point three microns in size.

It's a snug fit, it goes right around her face, up to the bridge of the nose and the tops of the cheekbones, and because it seems solid, she stops talking. Though if you can breathe through it, you ought to be able to talk through it. She secures it with Velcro pads at the back, seals herself up in front with the nose clip – shapes the clip to the nose. She's all stiff and hard now.

I look in the cocktail cabinet mirror. What I am looking at is us. We are a close-knit Dalston family – and we look a law unto ourselves, from a world of one-armed bandits in dim-lit cocktail lounges and topless waitresses . . . she could be presiding over the roulette, in that mask. Manny goes out and gets the captain's wheel off the hallway wall. The convex reflection looks like a surveillance installation.

Now you're ready to rob a bank, he says.

Just what I was thinking.

The kids look in the captain's wheel at their own bulging

comic faces next to hers. Or what can be seen of hers – with only the eyes peering out from under the dark fringe.

Could someone snap us, just like this, says Ossie. No leave it on, it'll be our Christmas card. Manny gets the camera, puts it on timer and steps back into the family group. With Paul back from South Africa we're a quorum: Manny and me and the kids; Paul, in the middle; Clive, the youngest; and Clive's part-ner Ossie. Who've I left out. Aneurin, the eldest, is in the States.

She makes a remark, faintly heard. You don't like it.

It's not that, says Manny. It's what it says. You might be bringing something on yourself.

Sadistic looking, says Clive. It's that metal piece over the bridge of the nose.

And the colour, says Ossie. Did you have to get it in black?

They only had it in black.

Well, you might just excite someone to a pre-emptive attack, Ossie says. When they see you coming like that and they don't know where you're coming from.

She looks at Clive with her bloodshot eyes – the mask pulling down the skin – to see if he agrees with Ossie. He usu-ally does.

He does. I don't know, he says.

Your mother roaming around Hackney in a black mask, says Ossie. Being a local character. As if we don't have enough of those.

What's one more then? I say. I don't see the problem.

They could at least have the courtesy to wait until she's left the room to talk about her. Local character. And after she's just bought the thing. Normally she'd be taking it off now and looking at it, thinking about taking it back – she's never quite sure about anything.

Thirty-one pounds, she says, hands hovering to take it off. That's with the replacement filter. Got it from a bike shop on the Holloway Road.

Bike shop, Manny says. You could get a bike.

Or she could jog. Ossie reads: jogging, skateboarding, climbing.

What? I say, jog back from Safeway with her shopping bags?

If she would ride a bike it wouldn't look so daft, says Manny.

Her hands come down. Everybody says *What?*

Whatever she is saying she has to say it again before she can make herself understood.

Isn't that what you really think? I know what she's saying. It's funny I can hear, but they can't.

She has to lift her mask or pull it away from the lower half of her face to speak down her chin. That's what you really think – *daft.*

She gets up. That's it, she's had enough. She's making ready to go out. Once it's on, it's on.

How will you tell people you want a dozen oranges? asks Clive, almost plaintive.

She points.

Once it's on, it's on, I say for her.

What if you can't point?

She'll need a slate, I say. Who did I give one to last Christmas? One like that.

Writing device, says Clive again. Now you really will be ready to rob a bank. Wouldn't it be simpler just to get something from your doctor for your asthma?

Her bloodshot eyes turn on him.

Someday, I say in conciliatory vein, we'll have our air cleaned up, like they do in Holland. We'll have trams and bicycle lanes . . .

Our royals don't ride bikes, she says. If they did, may be something would be done about cleaning up the air. She raises her mask to say that, and as she does, the mask pulls down the skin and exposes a little more of the red of her eyes. Wild-eyed republican, Ossie says.

The next time I dropped the kids with her for a couple of hours while I went to have my colour chart done, I wondered if I hadn't lived with this look long enough. I walked into the house on Amhurst Road, big run-down house. Was this pasty Edith Piaf look something I was born with? Was it handed down in packets of genes? Looking in the hall mirror, I saw her mask where she'd folded it with her gloves and scarf on the top shelf so the kids couldn't get to it and start playing cops and robbers. She would put it on just to walk to our house, three minutes away but on the other side of the heavy traffic of Kingsland Road.

She had started wearing earphones, so now she had two things around her head – she had a Walkman as well. Whenever I wanted to hear what she was listening to, she would relinquish the phones for a few seconds. One time it was Cassandra Wilson. I started to hand them back then hung on . . . Oh, *shit*. Wilson just poured into 'You Don't Know What Love Is'. I handed her the phones and she took them and put them on, couldn't wait to escape back to it.

She was miles away, and getting through to her became more difficult, what with the mask keeping other people out and the music keeping her in. She made a thing of how lost to the world she was, and when she went out, had a way of pulling down the skin to reveal red swimming eyeballs, as if to say it would be easier, wouldn't it, if she was just left alone?

The idea had been protection against the traffic fumes but now getting run over seemed some kind of danger. How was she to hear the screeching of brakes when a track she had on tape sounded like geese landing on the M25 with the skid of cars and lorries braking. It was a sax. Her musical taste was changing. She used to like Nat Cole. Or me, playing the vibes. Everything was soft, once. What is this music? I wanted to know. She said a name. Pharaoh something. Like the kings of Egypt.

I have to shoot off now, she said, putting on her mask, as if she had to be somewhere.

The kids complained she'd taken out the telly and put it in the box room – not very nice for them. And put her old electric piano in its place in the front room, where she would sit for hours with the phones on, working out chords, singing breathy scraps, or so I heard when I went round to pick them up. But I soon stopped leaving them there altogether. She didn't watch them. They could be getting up to anything.

She didn't sit with them in front of the telly, like she used to do. She didn't sneak up behind them and surround them with little hugs. They hardly knew they had a grandmother any more, she did not putter, or any of those little things, or the big things either. Her Sunday dinner was getting to be a thing of the past.

And when she did lay on something of a meal, it would be mostly foods of convenience. One Sunday we noticed she had completely forgotten to include a protein. I was searching the cooker. Hey! I could hear Paul's yelp as he went to look for her.

Oh, I'm sorry, I could hear, didn't I say? She was getting ready to go out. She had got herself a black sock cap, initially with a big pom-pom at the top. Which might have added a lighter touch, except that the pom pom had been removed. Somebody took it off in the tube, she said. She probably took it off herself. Didn't fit the new image.

What happened to your pom-pom, Mum?

Jean? Paul tried again. She didn't answer to that either. No hard feelings but she didn't want to pull her mask out of place just for the sake of chit chat.

She was out the door.

Where you going this time of a Sunday? Paul called after her.

Pub.

Which pub?

She didn't say.

Well it's the one time of the week the family gets together! Paul shouted after her, then said it again quietly to no one in particular, shuffling about. Suddenly the family was important to everyone but her.

One night I follow her to the Duke of Wellington. I don't actually follow her, but I kind of think that's where she's gone, probably because I heard her mention Balls Pond Road.

She's in the middle of a set. She takes her time, releasing herself into each phrase a little over-cautiously, I think at first, then I see what they're doing, she and her live electronics, a middle-aged keyboard player unknown to me. How they're working it, she fades in and out, as if she's singing from far away. 'You'd Be So Nice To Come Home To', a sound of coming through woods on a wintry night. And when the wind dies down, odd words of hers come through. When the wind picks up you lose her. It sounds like something done in a studio, the way she's fading in and out, but she's doing that with her voice. I'm impressed.

I take a sip of red wine. I sit in the dark and listen and when the set is over, I feel a little shy of crashing her party. I go round to leave. The Duke of Welly has a centre bar; I go out by the far side. Still, I think I ought to say hello maybe, turn back, but see she's with someone, or anyway sitting at the bar with someone. She's not the one doing the talking. He's talking, she's listening. I move around, down to the end by the door, and I can see she's laughing with her head thrown back and he has his hand on her leg, maybe to keep her from falling backwards, maybe not.

I don't know why, I shouldn't have done, but before I know it I'm telling Manny. She was great.

He looks a little aloof. Great? In what way?

I tell him how she sounded, how she looked and that there was a guy, a man. I'm telling him she's almost in white face. But far from trying for a remake she's the same but she's made some musical changes. Telling him what she sang. How techno things were. She had somebody new with her, referring to the keyboard player. Or, new to me. And then I realize he's not interested in the music, what she sang. He wants to know what the bloke looked like.

What bloke?

The bloke. Her boyfriend.

Huge mistake, saying anything. He keeps asking. Probably because I didn't bother to wipe the smile off my face when I walked in the door. We are in Paul's part of the house, his flat at the top, where we used to live, before we moved to the other house. Paul is down in her kitchen seeing if there's anything to eat down there.

What did he look like? Manny wants to know.

Nice face, I say. Dark.

What, Afro-Caribbean?

The whole thing under scrutiny now.

Sorry I spoke.

He thinks I'm playing games.

The old order changeth, I say. Manny wants his mother to stay put. I'd think you'd be pleased. She's re-invented herself.

I thought you said nothing's changed.

You know what I mean.

As we argue this – and what we are arguing about I do not know – I notice him looking closely not at me but at my face. I know what he's going to say. You're wearing too much make-up. He runs his finger across my cheek and holds it up as if there's make-up dripping off the end. But I'm not sitting here. I'm going down to put the kids in the car, I tell him.

I go downstairs to collect them. I'm in her bedroom. I notice the mask lying on the bed. Some of the black has faded. She's gone out without it. Some of the newness has gone out as well. It's not as stiff. It's crumpled on the bed like a shed skin.

Lunch-time

Sheena Joughin

THE DOOR WAS jammed half-open by now and the tables strewn at odd angles to each other with splayed spaces in between, where drink-limp legs in pressed denim ended in immaculate trainers, or were female and slender and evenly tanned; well-oiled, shiny, waxed and smooth.

'I want something sickly and sweet that will make me fat,' she told the lean face that was straining into hers, across the lobster-pink of their tablecloth, rather than me, although I was the waitress, breathing in her body lotion. 'Let's share something naughty.'

His fingers slid over her Rolex into the sleeve of her blouse.

'Let's be gross. Let's have a sticky toffee pudding.'

I looked away in case they kissed. They'd already been feeding each other king prawns, and she'd slipped off her sandals to put her feet between his. They were always like this at the end. She wouldn't eat something sweet if he paid her. He would be paying of course. I decided there wasn't anything left for dessert. We'd run out, I said flatly. Did they want coffee or just the bill? She looked at me then with something like hatred, but I chewed the gum we affected and smiled, sickly and sweet.

'I'll bring coffee, shall I? And a sugar bowl too?'

She knew I didn't like her. If she'd been with a woman she could have turned nasty, but her companion said how nice and the bill, if I would. He'd had enough foreplay clearly. Back at the dull wide sweep of the bar, Alison was lounging into Dusty, who was spilling complimentary peanuts over the cut-

61

lery she was supposed to be wrapping in napkins. Their arms were intertwined. She must have realised she was irritating me because she offered to take over the love-birds' bill, and one for Mary too, although she was in no state to pay at present. Mary came every lunch-time and fell asleep about halfway down her second bottle of house red, by which time her cheeks were finely veined with the same colour as her glass. We usually let her snooze on through the afternoon. She'd only be back at five twenty-five if we woke her up to go home.

I turned Ella Fitzgerald over and gave Dusty a drink on the house, to show I didn't mind him being there, and then I went talk to Suzanne and Jasper, so Alison wouldn't think I was intent on her man. I needed a cigarette anyway, and they'd just been to France, so had hundreds. They were slouched at table three, by the open back window, where they always sat at lunch-time. Suzanne was finishing up her second apple crumble, scratching at the plate with a teaspoon, complaining that it was her birthday and she'd only got two cards.

'I'm forty-three,' she told the room. 'I might as well be a hamster, for all the notice anyone takes.'

Jasper put his arm around my shoulder, and his hand on hers and his mouth against my ear to whisper that I must bring some champagne.

'Forty-three. I'll probably have a hot flush in a minute. Forty-bloody-three.' She thought she'd have another crumble if there were any left, but I was needed by a red-striped shirt at table six who called over to me to excuse him, so I went and leant over bleeding steaks and cigar butts to smile, curious, determinedly eager.

'I need more sex,' the one who hadn't called me explained to his thumbnail. 'My energy levels are all messed up.' Then he looked up to me and said, 'Cheese?' and I caressed the whole of his face with 'Of course'. I lifted two empty bottles of Chablis by slipping my fingers into them and smiled widely at the space I'd made.

'Of course,' I indulged us, 'I'll see what we have.'

We had Stilton and Brie and Cheddar of course, which was what we had every day, but it's sometimes worthwhile for a waitress to seem confused by the choices her customers face.

My sister, Isa, who works at Temps Perdu too, is best at this fictional bewilderment, because she knows exactly what's in the fridge at any given time. She has a photographic memory, our father says. But she hadn't been in for ten days, which was why I was doing a lunch-time. Isa'd disappeared, everyone said, and some people were worried, but I was not, partly because she always knows exactly what's in the fridge. Ella sang that she had still a song in her heart and I whistled along like waiters in films do, and skimmed a full ashtray away to the bar-top that belonged to me for now, like these last replete customers all did too, in a way. Through the polish of our gold-lettered front window a bus was jammed roaring in traffic and a child stared out from the top deck, its palms pressed white to the glass.

I dropped pound coins into the till and ran the taps and had a gulp of my drink and replaced the Chablis men's ashtray and was asked for port and blushed out 'Of course' again. I found Jasper's champagne and an ice bucket too and I gave the lovers more coffee and said I did hope it was hot, then I took Mary's newspaper out of her uplifted hands, because she'd once set a Sunday supplement alight from a candle. I took smeared glasses to the kitchen, where the washer-upper was sitting on a counter sliding with dirty plates, eating cheesecake with a knife. He was new and Italian and handsome. His father was dying so he was going back to Lucca the next afternoon. I asked him if he wanted a drink and he did, so I went to find one, collecting money from tables as I travelled. I assessed the sturdy porcelain tip jar which was a satisfying weight. I poured myself another drink, along with Antonio's, and watched the rust-coloured geraniums in the window-box quiver to the vibrations of the Shepherd's Bush Road.

'Three-thirty,' said Dusty. 'Lock-up time, Chrissie,' so I reached the long brass keys from their cleaning-cloth cupboard hide-out as Ella decided that this couldn't be love because she felt so well. She sounded as if she really did too. The woman who hated me left with her man and her sling-backs and her miniature handbag and I went to round up the necks of their empties and found four pound coins under a saucer. Alison must have admired his tie. She was good at that sort of thing, since she'd been in love. I nudged tables into symmetry along the grubby sanded floor that was puddled with September sun. I picked up damp fragments of green paper napkins and someone's address and telephone number, that was folded and soft like sat-on warm grass, then I took the worn rubber wedge from underneath the plate-glass door. I was twisting the dangled cardboard sign to the side that said 'Closed' when I found my face in front of a checked shirt that I'd bought at a jumble sale about five years before. It was Nick, who I hadn't seen for months, unless you count dreaming. The door was half-open. It was twenty to four.

'Isa's not here.'

I should have just said hello and not mentioned her name, because it was there then, in the room, like a broken floorboard you have to step over.

'I'm doing Isa's shifts for her all this week.' Not looking at him at all, but at the air outside, as if it might be about to rain something strange, and with the door handle still in my first like a knife. The same bus was stuck in the traffic, and there was a siren out there too now, with a flashing light frenetic and blocked. The child I'd seen before was still in the top of the bus, still staring and pressing the oblong glass. It was three forty and Nick was here at the wine bar and there was suddenly nothing to say. If it was a dream we'd be kissing. I must not look at his mouth.

'She's not here, if that's what you wanted.' My face was probably sweaty and red. I hadn't washed my hair for three days. I must have smelled of grease and smoke and meat. He smelled the same as he always did – like a launderette with a bread oven in it.

'Are we too late for leftovers even?' A girl behind him stepped forward to ask. She was taller than us and she knew my name.

'I'm Lily, Chrissie.' She held out her hand at about my breast level. 'I wanted to buy this man something to eat. He's been lifting boxes for me all morning.' She had an Australian accent. The music in the room behind me stopped and I held the door and listened to traffic and police car and laughter and Suzanne's voice above it saying, 'You can't be. You were older than that when we met.' Then Jasper was beside me with his bleary breath and his arm around my waist, as if I was a bus-stop late at night.

'Nick,' he said. 'Nick, for Christ's sake. Now we really do need a drink. And it's Suzanne's birthday. More drinks all round. More drink for the birthday girl, Chrissie.'

I couldn't say we were supposed to be closed because Suzanne was with us now too, going on about being forty-three, and no need to tell everyone and Jasper saying he thought she wanted attention and no, she said, she wasn't a child, for God's sake and then more insistence from him that we must all have a drink and her asking Nick if Jasper looked younger than she did.

'Forty-bloody-three, Nick.' She had her hand in his. 'How old are you anyway?'

'Same age as Chrissie, however old that is.'

I dropped the door handle and I went to the Ladies', and started at the mirror where I seemed swollen and pink. I drank some water from the tap but that made it worse because my mouth came out a different shape. I took my pulse, which was eighty-three, and I thought of climbing away through the window of the Gents' to the garden next door, but that would not be reasonable. I should go back and be polite but distant and leave. To disappear would seem hysterical. As if I just wanted attention.

When I came out they were all sitting at table three, which was oval with a flat end where a drop-leaf was missing. Dusty was leaning into the wall behind Lily, making a framed Matisse print hang at an angle because of his shoulder. Alison was filling her purse up with tips and said she'd got to go to the dentist's but would be back at five to open up.

'Leave it a mess, when you leave,' she said, 'I've been useless. Dusty kept me up all night.' She called to him that he had to come but he said no, he'd hang round and catch her later, so she went and took his hand and had a word in his ear. He decided to go after all.

'Putty,' said Jasper, as Nick turned the key behind them. 'That man is a changed man, I'll tell you.'

'It's love,' said Suzanne. 'You couldn't understand.'

I went to the kitchen with Antonio's wine and I stayed there for a while, being gesturally helpful, while he talked about his father, but I couldn't listen because of Nick being upstairs and wanting to go there, but not wanting him to have me there, in case that was what he wanted. In the end I asked Antonio to come up with me for a drink. I could pretend I was in love with him if the worst came to the worst. If this was not the worst already.

'I dwell in possibility,' I said to myself for some reason. I asked Antonio if he'd heard of Emily Dickinson, as if I were indeed in love with him, and then I said that it was his last day, which he seemed to find confusing.

'I mean, it's your last day,' I said again, more loudly, although his English was perfect. 'We must leave all this for the night shift.' I took his arm, that was skinny like a loaf of French bread, and led him up past the others to the back of the bar and asked him what he'd like me to open. He chose Montbazillac, which threw me, because it was expensive, but the owner was in France for three weeks, and I'd be in Yorkshire by the time he got back so I thought I might as well. Isa would be around to explain everything next week. She took things she shouldn't all the time. She stole Nick from me when he'd always been mine. I don't know how she explained that to herself. At table six, Mary was snoozing with one hand on a glass. The yellow cardigan she never took off was rising and falling on the gentle swell of her front.

I dropped empties into the chute that smashed them down to the bins and thought how nice it would be to manage to sleep sitting up. You wouldn't ever have to face the emptiness of bed. Ella had started to sing 'Nice Work if You Can Get it', and Jasper was singing along then he suddenly stood up, as she paused for the piano to strain into the strings, and he took Suzanne's hands and there they were dancing – she clutching a wineglass-stem along with some of his fingers, and he with a dripping cigarette in his mouth. They were quite good together. They looked like a birthday; like a dodgem car making little jerked paths across the darkening floor, banging tables and knocking the bar, then finding a space again and swinging round inside it. He had a knee between her legs, to direct her, and a hand on the small of her back.

'Holding hands at midnight, 'neath the starry sky,' Suzanne sang, 'Nice work if you can get it, and if you get it, tell me how.' She couldn't sing in fact, and Jasper must have realised that because he stubbed his cigarette into a saucer in front of me and began to whistle, then he stopped and kissed her and they weren't dancing then but leaning into the bar about a foot away from me and I didn't know what to do exactly, so I turned the music off. It was four thirty-five; they carried on kissing and I should have cashed up by now. Perhaps I should leave it for Alison. She wouldn't have been drinking. Suzanne untangled from Jasper and went back to the group at the table to rub Nick's shoulders, talking over the back of his head to Lily, who was twenty-three and had just rented a house boat to stay on 'til Christmas. Nick was smoking, drinking the sweet wine that Antonio had put beside him, but they weren't talking. I opened the till and stared at the notes folded round each other and the coins in all the wrong places.

Then the phone rang. Nick stood up as I answered it and it was Isa, in a phone box that she couldn't make work. The little beeping noises went on through her saying 'Hello,' then she hung up, then it rang again. I turned my back to the room and said no, he wasn't there. No, Nick had not been in. Just the regulars and Suzanne's birthday.

'But he said to ring him at half three there today. Is it much after that?' I said yes, it was nearly five, but nothing else. Jasper took a twenty-pound note from his trouser pocket and wanted more champagne. I jerked my head towards the fridge. He swayed in towards it and stared at the side-on bottles, very puzzled, not pulling any out. The phone beeped and Isa inserted more money.

'I don't understand. He said he'd be there.'

'Perhaps he changed his mind. He's been known to do that.'

Silence. More beeps and another coin forcing through.

'Has that girl Lily been in?'

'Are you still pregnant?' I shouldn't have asked that. It made me feel sick.

'Not really. I mean no, I'm not. Tell him that if he does come in will you?'

'I wouldn't speak to Nick if you paid me, Isa. Or you either in fact.'

I put the phone down. It rang again so I picked it up but unplugged it with my left hand and kept it to my ear for some time in case anyone was watching. Then I left it and slid a bottle of Veuve Cliquot from under some water and handed it to Jasper.

'Let's get drunk. I'm clocking off,' I said, and I took down a proper champagne glass and went to sit between Nick and Lily, on the chair with the short leg.

Antonio was telling Suzanne that his father might not die. He said it reassuringly, as if it was her parent at stake rather than his. She told the glass in her hand that her father had died three years ago in Ireland in a caravan, but she hadn't cared because she hated him. Jasper said that was silly because nobody simply hates their father. Although his mother had certainly hated his now that he thought about it. Suzanne said that that was silly. Nobody hates their husband unless they hated their father, which was why she'd hated her last one, if she thought about it properly.

'He wasn't worth hating, in himself,' she explained, drawing little round faces with smiles on them on the table with spilled fizz. 'He was fond of me. It wasn't his fault we didn't get on. It wasn't just his fault at all.' As if I had said it must have been. It seemed to be me she was talking to now. 'But I wouldn't let him be nice to me. Do you see what I mean? He was nice, though. Really he was.' She had her hand on Jasper's leg, playing with the soft grey fabric there. 'I was fond of him, too. He was kind, you know? A very kind man. Good with children.' She took a full glass of sweet wine, which was foolish, because she'd been drinking champagne until then. Jasper crossed his legs away from her hand with a jerk.

'He'd have had to be good with children to get along with you,' he said. He was slurring his speech. 'All men have to be good with children, if they want to get laid.'

Lily stopped lighting a Marlboro to stare at him. She looked like she'd just seen someone being mugged. He went on regardless: 'What do you think, Nick? How are you with babies?'

'Nick's having a baby. Didn't you know?' Suzanne's eyes glinted. Her dress was off her shoulder. She had a black bra on.

'He's not,' I said. It was the first thing I had said, and I said it directly at Nick, who was buttoning his top button up, looking down, giving his fine chin lots of little underneath wrinkles. He seemed to not be listening, so I said it again.

'Nick is not having a baby,' I said.

'Thank God for that,' said Jasper. 'What's happened to the music?' He fumbled up, focusing towards the bar, where the cassette deck's little blue light seemed exceptionally bright. I didn't know you could see it from table three.

'Who was that on the phone?' Nick was talking into my eyes now. 'Who was ringing up before?'

I told him a customer. Two customers, I said. Two men who wanted big tables. I touched the top of his head while I talked to him because I was drunk and he said I was drunk and should have some juice.

'I'm not a child,' I said and then there was Aretha Franklin very loudly going to knock on his door and tap on his window-pane, with the back-up girls sighing in time and Mary was awake and humming along. I'd never seen her do that before. She still had her eyes closed, but was holding her glass up. I hoped Jasper wouldn't ask her to dance. I felt like dancing myself. Then there was a real knocking from across the room and we all turned to see Dusty with Alison outside the door, holding hands, pressing their noses to the glass, squashing a bunch of flowers between them. It was five fifteen. Jasper swayed from behind the bar to let them in, saying, 'A bouquet for the birthday girl.' Then Suzanne was weeping all at once, wishing her mother was here again between sobs, but nobody took any notice, because a woman came in with a bleeding-faced baby and a purse in her mouth and a half unfolded pushchair. She wanted to use the phone. She'd slipped off the bus, she shouted over the music, and the baby had hit the pavement. The baby was screaming and Antonio was wetting napkins from the tap at the bar, which he left running as he rushed to the child's smeary face, that it was rubbing little fists into by now. Alison tried the phone which of course was dead, since I had unplugged it and she kept saying 'It's broken,' so I stood up to go over and noticed a moment when everything seemed to stand still, with a gap in the music and Jasper holding his flowers and the sun making some sugar that was on the floor shine, and then Lily was on her feet and out through the door and back again, taking the accident with her.

'There's a taxi outside,' she explained to us all. 'We'll take it to Charing Cross. She'll get there fastest in a cab.' Then she'd gone and the middle of the room was empty, and Alison was taking bottles from our table and nobody said anything, until Nick said he couldn't go anywhere now because he had Lily's keys in his pocket. We didn't quite know why Lily had gone, or if she would ever come back. Suzanne and Jasper said it was nicest here anyway and Antonio decided to stay and wash up some more. Dusty had a brandy, because of the blood, which had made him feel faint he said. Alison's mouth was numb so she had to have one too. Tuesday nights were quiet as a rule, but I laid some tables anyway and bulked up the high fridge with white wine and water. I could have gone somewhere else whenever I wanted. Alison gave me my wages and most of the tips. She must have felt guilty, or sorry for me. I bought a bottle of wine and put it in front of Nick and Suzanne and felt dizzy but took a full glass.

'You see,' Suzanne was telling the table. 'You see, anything can happen. People have accidents. I nearly died when I fell off my bicycle once.'

'You're a long time dead,' said Jasper, like he always did, when he was about this drunk. Then he said Suzanne couldn't ride a bicycle, as far as he knew, and she said she could and I asked Nick if he'd like to get married.

'Shall we get married?' I said, 'In case.'

'In case what?' he said. But he didn't say no, so I took his wrist and kept it for hours through the changing light and the night arriving and talk about bicycles and birthdays and drinking and each other and the people we saw but didn't know and when he left, at nearly midnight, I went back all the wavy way to his front door. And then he did say no.

'You can't stay, Chrissie. You can't.'

'But I can't get home.'

70

'I'll call you a cab.' So we went in together through rooms that I used to live in and we stood side by side as he rang for a taxi. There were three messages flashing on his answering machine. It didn't seem worth touching his back while I was there, but as soon as I was in the taxi I wished that I had, so when I got out I paid the man and I ran all the way back to where I'd just come from, which took nearly half an hour. It was a foolish thing to do, because he seemed scared rather than impressed with my need and called another taxi right away. I wouldn't get into that one though. I said I hoped he died sorry, which I took back the next morning, and I walked away, in a different direction, towards the shine of Charing Cross Road. I moved quickly along glossed pavement, walking too near the kerb, then changed to inside everyone else to be safe, then turned off to the left, along past the noise of a party to make a short zig-zag to the steps of Suzanne's front door. She was wearing her coat and toasting bread, and glad to have someone to share it with since Jasper was asleep in a chair.

'That's the trouble with men,' she said, putting a cigarette between buttery lips. She smoked instead of explaining it to me.

'What is?'

'What?'

'The trouble with men?'

'Well, they don't want enough, do they? That's why we live longer, you see. They just don't want enough.'

Biting the Cord

Andrew Dempster

TUBE DRIVERS RAN OVER INJURED DOG TO AVOID DELAYS

London Underground ordered four trains to pass over a dog lying on the track to avoid causing rush-hour delays, it admitted yesterday.

The incident began at 7.07 am when the driver of a Northern Line train in the tunnel near Highgate station hit something on the track. He walked back and found the dog, then radioed to control and was told to continue.

A second train at 7.10 am was ordered to proceed over the dog. The next two trains were also forced to drive over the dog and at 7.28 am two managers who happened to be at Highgate went to the scene. One muzzled the dog by wrapping his coat around it and lifted it into the cab of another train, which took it to East Finchley. The RSPCA was contacted at 7.36 am, arrived at 8.47 am and the dog was destroyed at 8.51 am.

A spokesman for the transport union RMT said staff had been 'very distressed' by the incident but added: 'It is standard practice for London Underground to proceed when a dog is injured. Drivers who do not obey are usually disciplined and sent home.'

—(extract) Carol Midgley, *The Times*, Thursday, 2 May, 1996

48 The Green
Southgate London N14 3BB

1/5/96

Dear Mum,

Thanks for your letter. It arrived on Tuesday. It's good to hear that you are settling in to your new place and that you are feeling better. It certainly sounds like the Greek man at the fish shop is a real character and I was pleased to hear that you are starting to make friends.

Unfortunately, things are not going as well with me. A nasty thing happened to me today and I thought I had better write to you. I hit a dog driving my train. That looks silly now I've written it down, like the dog was driving the train. It might be funny too if it wasn't so sad. I stopped the train and went back to see how it was and it was lying between the tracks in a pretty bad shape. It wouldn't let me come near it. It was snapping and growling and it was pretty big. It looked like a German Shepherd. I went back and radioed and they told me to drive on. I found out later that three more trains went over him before they picked him up. Three more trains. They put him down in the manager's room at East Finchley. I feel really bad about it, especially with the others going over him like that. He was in a lot of pain already without having four trains run over him. He was scared, too, but I couldn't help him. He was trying to bite me – he was really scared.

You know how much I love driving trains, but when something like this happens, I wonder if I should be doing something else. Working on the tube was a dream I had as a kid, but does that mean it is the right thing for me to do? Today I killed a dog just doing my job. What sort of job is it where you kill animals and not worry about it?

I wish you were still here to talk to about things like this, Mum. I hope that you are feeling better and all that Sydney sun is treating you well. From your last letter it sounds like it is.

I'll write a longer letter later. I just wanted to tell you about the dog.

Lots of love,
Brian

PERFORMANCE CHECK

This graph shows how each Underground line and the Underground as a whole performed against its targets for service regularity, expressed in percentage terms for comparison. Information on performance against other targets is contained in a leaflet available from the ticket office.

If you have been delayed for 15 minutes or more through our fault, you are entitled to a refund. Details and a claim form are contained in our Customer Charter in the leaflet rack at any station.

4 WEEKS ENDING FRIDAY 29 MARCH 1996

Bakerloo (target 95.0)	94.1
Central (target 96.8)	95.7
Circle and Hammersmith and City (target 94.5)	94.6
District (target 93.5)	93.8
East London	Line Closed
Jubilee (target 98.5)	97.9
Metropolitan (target 96.7)	96.9
Northern (target 95.0)	92.8
Piccadilly (target 97.0)	94.9
Victoria (target 95.8)	97.2
Waterloo and City (target 96.8)	99.0
Network (target 95.7)	94.9

Train service regularity is measured by timing the intervals between trains. If the time between trains is twice the scheduled interval or more this counts as a failure to meet the target. The East London Line is closed for engineering work.

—poster, Archway station,
6/5/1996

77

Sir,

I was incensed by the article 'Tube drivers ran over injured dog to avoid delays' (2 May). Has London Underground gone mad? This dedication to their Customer Charter is ridiculous. Surely the majority of their 'customers', as they choose to call their passengers, would be outraged to hear of such a thing. A few minutes extra delay for a humane act is not too much to ask. Such delays are absolutely usual on the Northern Line which is constantly dogged by breakdowns of equipment and limited service. Most passengers would not have noticed the difference.

I fear that such happenings are symptoms of a broader disregard that is creeping into the British way of thinking. In the same way that a dog can be run over several times in the name of efficiency, we are now slaughtering thousands of cattle in the name of restoring confidence in a market. Even those that argue against the slaughter are doing so on behalf of the farming industry. What about the cows? They are herbivores. They were never meant to eat offal in the first place. BSE is a result of an unseemly haste to get a cheap product on to the supermarket shelf. However, that product was once a sentient being. We British pride ourselves that we are animal lovers. But that pride is a sick and misplaced joke.

Infuriated, Hampstead

TUBE DRIVERS SEES "GHOST DOG"

Brian Slaven, the London Underground driver whose train hit a dog last week – leading to a controversial incident in which three subsequent trains were ordered to drive over the injured animal to avoid delays – was given two weeks' sick leave yesterday after he claimed to have seen the dog's ghost.

Mr Slaven said he saw a large dog running in front of his train near Oval station on the Northern Line. He stopped the train at 9.54 am and walked forward in the train's lights but the dog had disappeared. After he reported the incident to his superior, he was instructed to take a break from driving.

A London Underground spokesperson said that incidents such as last week's 'put an unnecessary strain on drivers and in the interests of safety a brief rest is usually suggested in cases like this'.

—(extract) *Independent*,
Friday, 10 May, 1996

Patient: Brain Slaven, Driver   15/5/96

Background: Hit dog on track near Highgate 1/5. Three further trains also ran over dog before dog removed and destroyed. Patient distressed as consequence. Claimed to see similar dog on track near Oval 9/5. Given two weeks' leave by supervisor.

Interview: Feels guilty for hitting dog. Expressed reservations regarding his own motivations for driving trains and for LU policy re animals. Most adamant that second dog was not imagined. Expressed strong but conflicting desires both to continue work and to take leave. Desire to continue work seems to arise from fear that LU looks unfavourably on dog sighting. Reassured him strongly on this point.

Recommendation: Stress very evident. Would benefit from extension of leave to four weeks.

—London Underground occupational counselling service
officer's notes

Dear Brian,

Thanks for your letter. I'm writing straight back because you sounded so upset (and also because now you owe me a letter!). I was really sorry to hear about the dog. You must be feeling terrible. I know just how it must be. It's just like when your father ran over Sammy. You boys never really forgave him but you never stopped to think how he felt about it. He was heartbroken. He loved that dog just as much as you did, and killing him, with you and Ron all upset, was almost too much for him. I'm not saying that what happened to you is the same, but if you are feeling sorry, spare a thought for him that's not with us. He loved you, too.

It's a sad thing that the dog had to die, but driving a train you're bound to hit things. You can't go taking the blame for that. It's just life (and death if you want to think of it that way) going about its business. It's sad but it's the way of the world. Cheer up, lad, and try and put it behind you.

I've been finding my way around Sydney pretty well. In some ways, it's just a big city like London. I went over to Manly on the ferry last week with Mrs Spencer. It was lovely going on the Harbour, and Manly is a very nice beach, much bigger than Coogee. Mrs Spencer was just recovering from an operation. She had been in the Prince of Wales Hospital for three weeks having a lump taken out of her neck. She's got a nasty row of stitches to show for it, but she was back at bowls yesterday just like she was never ill. Well, I'll stop writing now before I need a new piece of paper.

Love Mum

48 The Green
Southgate London N14 3BB

18/5/96

Dear Mum,
Thanks again for your letter. Your trips around Sydney
sound very interesting. In fact, all that time spent at the seaside
makes it sound like a holiday. You must be very pleased.
Speaking of holidays, I'm off work at the moment. A few
strange things have happened since I last wrote. One day last
week as I was driving my train, it was about a week after I hit
the dog, I saw a dog about the same size running ahead of my
train. The papers said it was the ghost of the dog I hit but I
never thought that. It was another dog, about the same size. It
was on a different section of track, down by Oval station. I
stopped and got out but it had run away. I told them at control
and they reported it. They gave me 2 weeks off. Then I saw the
psychologist and he made it 4 weeks. I think they think I'm
going a bit nuts. It's such a long time – I'm sure it's more than I
need. If it hadn't happened so quickly, I could have treated it
like a holiday. I've just been kicking my heels around the house.
I dug out that old hydrangea that you planted when we moved
in – it was diseased and all its new leaves were covered in
brown spots. I planted some annuals along the front fence and
they seem to be doing well. And I fertilised everything for
summer.
Another funny thing that happened was to do with a dog
as well. I was coming back from Harry's place on the
Metropolitan Line last Sunday and I was sitting looking at this
dog. It was a nice enough Jack Russell, just sitting peacefully as
we left Finchley Road station. Then, as we approached Baker
Street, it started looking around, getting agitated. Once
we went underground, it growled and strained at the leash,
eyeballing me. Then it started barking, getting really wild. I
was getting scared at this point. It would have bitten me if the
owner hadn't held it back. It was as if it knew I had run that
other dog down, like they were friends or something. In the end,
the owner got really worried and took him straight off the train.

It was so strange. I'm sure it was something to do with going underground. He was fine outside. Something's going on, Mum. Ever since it happened, whenever I go underground, I get a nervous feeling on my neck, like someone or something is about to touch me.

Anyway, with all this time off I've been thinking about whether I'm doing the right thing with my life and all that. Running over that dog has made me wonder whether I really want to drive trains. I get the feeling that maybe you did the right thing going out there. It would be pretty easy for me to throw it all in here and go out as well. The change would do me good, like it did for you, don't you think? Let me know if you think this is a good idea.

Missing you,
Brian

P.S. There are some letters here from your insurance company and from the Gardening Society. Do you want me to open them or forward them on?

Duty Station Manager
Bank and Monument Stations
London Underground
Threadneedle St
London EC2 9BB

21 May 1996

Mrs Georgina Jennings
Coordinator, Station Services
London Underground Limited
55 Broadway
London SW1H 0BD

Dear Georgina,

I refer to our telephone conversation of today, regarding several incidents involving dogs that have recently occurred at this station. The three incidents can be summarised as follows:

1. On Saturday, 18 May, a customer lost control of her spaniel on the descending escalator on the Central Line. The dog leapt from her arms and bit into another customer's expensive shirt. The shirt was badly torn, but no other item of clothing was damaged. More importantly, however, the dog managed to grab hold of a chain that was beneath the shirt and attached to rings piercing the customer's nipples and naval. All three rings were torn out, causing the customer some serious discomfort. Apparently he is seeking legal advice as to whether London Underground has been negligent.

2. A dog was sighted by a driver of the Waterloo and City service on Thursday, 16 May. He slowed the train and followed, or chased, this dog past the end of the platform at Bank station. In the tunnel, the dog turned on him and stood its ground, growling. The driver could see that it was protecting a litter of very young pups. He returned to the train and radioed control.

He was advised to wait for me to come and assess the situation. When I arrived, we both entered the tunnel but after searching both the tunnel and the reversing siding, we found that the dog and pups were gone, although their paw prints were visible on the sleepers. There have been no further reports of them anywhere in the station.

3. This morning, after staff opened Monument station at around 6.20 am, an inspection of the platform revealed a series of no less than seven mounds of dog mess. The station had been locked as usual prior to being opened, and an interview with the supervisor of the night cleaning staff confirmed that the platform was clean when the station was locked around 1.50 am. The suggestion that it may be the dog sighted at Bank seems unlikely since this dog had left no previous evidence and would suddenly have produced a great volume. However, no other explanation has been put forward.

I hope this provides the information you are seeking. If you have any further queries, please do not hesitate to call again.

Best regards,
Arthur Stratford
Duty Station Manager

TUBE GOES TO THE DOGS

London Underground's recent problems with dogs worsened yesterday when a pack of hounds prevented a train from stopping at Baker Street station. The station was subsequently closed for over an hour.

As the Hammersmith and City Line train approached the station, the driver became suspicious about the absence of people on the platform. The group of some forty dogs then appeared and charged towards him. The driver claimed that they appeared to be 'completely wild' and charged the train as it passed, rebounding from the windows.

Concerned for the safety of his passengers, the driver accelerated away, stopping at Edgware Road station, which has an open-air platform. Above-ground and open-air platforms are thought to be safer than underground platforms involved in the recent series of dog-related incidents.

In the past three weeks, over three hundred complaints and incidents involving dogs have been recorded by London Underground. Complaints have ranged from a handful of minor attacks to a much larger number describing incidents of dogs contaminating London Underground property. Yesterday's incident was the first attack by a pack of dogs.

A spokesperson said that London Underground management was 'very concerned' about the increasing number of incidents involving dogs. Measures being considered include the banning of dogs from travelling on the tube and the hiring of part-time dog catchers.

— *Independent*,
Friday, 24 May, 1996

FROGGY DOGGY SAILS THE RAILS

London Underground went barking mad yesterday when Mittzy, a five-year-old French poodle, drove one of their trains right out of Waterloo station.

Two hours later, the Bakerloo Line train was seen coming out of the Channel Tunnel in Calais.

'She only wanted to go home,' said Mittzy's owner, Mrs Natalie Scilly of Kilburn, in tears. 'She's been off her food with all this BSE business. She's a Paris dog, really. We'll miss her terribly.'

'She took me off my guard,' said Harry Shortfield, the driver of the dognapped train. 'She came out of nowhere and pushed me out the door as I was looking down the platform at Baker Street.'

A tube spokesman said: 'First Cantona wins the Cup Final, now this. I say we ban Brie and garlic.'

—*Sunday Sport* front page,
26 May, 1996 (with photograph)

GROUND CANINES

Take the long escalator down at Holborn Underground station. You are ingested into the viscera of the city, drawn down to where we can no longer manipulate nature's rules. The long, slender throat slides you down into the belly of the dragon.

In London, they have always talked of 'braving the tube'. This self-conscious but offhand assertion of bravado has developed a new meaning in recent weeks, one far more sinister but also more accurate. As a reward for the simple act of bravery of waiting for a train, four people lay in hospital last week, victims of an unprecedented and increasingly widespread pattern of violence. Violence is not new to either London or London Underground, but violence perpetrated by dogs on London Underground — that is new.

As with other recent perceived threats to public safety, such as the Dunblane massacre and the BSE revelations, the authorities have proved impotent when charged with either explaining or dealing with the crisis. The paltry measures introduced by London Underground and the Metropolitan Police have not reduced the rate at which attacks are occurring. Effectively faced with securing their own safety, passengers have avoided the tube in droves, placing a huge burden on other means of transport, particularly London Transport buses. Traffic, already congested in central London, has reached intolerable levels with the number of reports of road rage leaping dramatically.

The crisis has highlighted the dependence of the city on its underground rail network. Of the one million people travelling into central London each day, 60% use the tube. Without it, London would cease to operate effectively, a fact that has not escaped the notice of the IRA in recent years. Elements of the ageing network, both stations and tunnels, are increasingly required to be repaired, leading to closures that seem to be becoming longer and more frequent. Passengers have patiently accepted these closures as being necessary for the future of the tube, and those due to the IRA as being a cross they have to bear, but there is frustration and anger at the growing number of closures due to dogs. Dog attacks were the cause of an average three tube station closures per day this week (with eight on Tuesday), averaging two and a half hours in length.

The 'plague' of dogs has no precedent in Underground history, although dogs, or at least their ghosts, have caused problems for mainline service operators. The most notable example was the infamous 'Bristol Bob' who haunted the Great Western Railway station at Bristol for decades at the end of last century. There was also the terrifying 'Black Shuck' at Waterloo station. Anyone sighting him was reputed to die within a year.

—(extract) 'Life' supplement to the *Observer*,
Sunday, 26 May, 1996

BEACH INSPECTORS

Inspectors required for Coogee beach. Early morning shift. Please send application and two references to: Staff Recruitment, Randwick Council, 257 Alison Rd, Randwick 2031.

—Classified section, *Sydney Morning Herald*, 25 May, 1996

4/74 Coogee Bay Rd
Coogee 2033 NSW
Australia
26/5/96

Dear Brian,

Thanks for your letter. It's nice to hear you've got some time off, but my advice to you is to be careful. Remember what happened to your Uncle Sid. They gave him a few weeks off so he could rest and he never worked again. I'm not saying you're going to end up in a home like he did but just make sure they mean it when they say they want you back. As far as I'm concerned, you should get right back to work as soon as you can. You have a hard think about your idea about coming out here to stay with me, as well. It's not that I don't want you to visit, that would be very nice, but I really think it's time you started standing up for yourself. You've got the house now, and your job if you don't go losing your grip. You don't want to be keeping company with an old stick like me. Find yourself a nice girl and settle down. I'm not in a hurry to be a grandmother but sometime before I die would be nice.

Anyway, if you do decide to come over, I've taken a little liberty and I've written to apply for a job on your behalf. An outdoor job with an early start so I'm sure you'll like it. I won't tell you what it is so it can be a surprise. I think you would be very disappointed with the railways here, son, so I can tell you now that it's not a railway job. I went into the city with Mrs Spencer and her son (he's unemployed – Mrs Spencer is trying to find him a job too) the other day on the railway from Bondi Junction. It is the nearest station to where I live and it is about five miles away! They don't have nothing like the tube. You stick with your job. You don't know how lucky you are.

Love Mum

48 The Green
Southgate London N14 3BB

3/6/96

Dear Mum,
Thanks for your letter. I've been thinking about what you said and I'm going to do it. I'm going back to work. I talked to Jerry and he agreed that I could go back this Thursday, 6th June. It's only three days away and I'm quite looking forward to it. What you said was right, Mum, I really did need to make some decisions about my life. Not that going out to be with you wouldn't be nice too, but I think I'll try and do my best here. I've bought myself a new pair of boots for the big day.

There is something that you need to know, though. Since I went on leave, the tube has become a much more dangerous place. I don't know if you've seen on the news over there but there have been some serious attacks by dogs in the Underground. They've had to close stations and everything. Only yesterday, Goodge Street, Marble Arch and Knightsbridge were all closed for a couple of hours because dogs were running wild on the platforms. A lot of the drivers are taking their leave and calling in sick so that's one reason they're keen for me to come back. People are scared, Mum. Every day someone ends up in hospital from a dog attack. I feel good about going back to work, but I'm a bit scared too. I know it sounds stupid, but I sometimes think if it wasn't for me hitting that dog none of this would have happened. That's another reason I have to go back. I can't let other people be at risk when it's my fault.

The garden hasn't really got going this year. Winter just doesn't seem to be ending. Strange things are happening like the irises are up early despite the fact it's still so cold that it snowed in Yorkshire last week. There's no explaining it, the way nature works.

Love Brian

DOGS KILL ON TUBE

After several weeks of problems associated with dogs, a canine-related human tragedy finally struck London Underground yesterday. In a violent attack, three dogs brought down a man and mauled him to death. The attack was so frenzied that witnesses were powerless to intervene in defence of the man, whose name has not been released.

The incident occurred late in the afternoon at the Underground station serving Heathrow Terminals 1,2,3. The man is believed to have been a steward who had been working on the KLM flight that arrived from Amsterdam at 3.45 pm. He had arrived at the Underground station around 50 minutes later. He was carrying no luggage except for a trolley bearing a small Samsonite suitcase. According to witnesses, a Piccadilly Line train had recently departed, leaving only about thirty people on the platform. The three dogs circled the man's luggage, at first simply sniffing it. According to observers, one dog then took the trolley and suitcase in its jaws, ripping open the suitcase. The others then joined in, leaving clothing and other personal items strewn along the platform. The man began screaming at the dogs which then turned on him. They swiftly overpowered him, dragging him to the ground and, in the words of one onlooker, 'tearing him to pieces'.

—(extract) *Guardian* (headline story),
Thursday, 6 June, 1996

(MB): Relief for London Underground today as, for the first time this week, no stations were closed to protect their passengers from dogs. The respite comes in the aftermath of yesterday's fatal attack at Heathrow. The attacks seem to have ceased as suddenly and mysteriously as they began, about two weeks ago. No sightings of dogs were reported anywhere on the Underground network today.

(TERRY MANNING, DUTY STATION MANAGER, NOTTING HILL GATE): Very relieved. It's very mysterious and we're not counting our chickens, but we've got our fingers crossed. A few more days like this and things will be back to normal, which will make everyone very happy.

(MB): A London Underground spokesperson said earlier today that stoppages caused by the dogs had cost London Underground around two million pounds in lost revenue and refund claims.

—transcript, *Nine O'Clock News*, BBC1,
Thursday, 6 June, 1996

COOGEE DOG PACK

A 'pack of dogs' stripped a beach inspector of his brand new uniform on Coogee beach early yesterday morning. The inspector, Henry Spencer, was on his first day in the job and blames the attack on his uniform. 'I looked too much like a postman,' he said, according to the surprised Beach Street resident who found the naked inspector on her doorstep.

—Column 8, *Sydney Morning Herald*,
8 June, 1996

Feathers in our Knickers

Louis de Bernières

MUCH TO THE dismay of my parents and friends, I was guilty in the past of deliberately not having a career. I suspect that my grounds were that I would never get old; the future was a long time off; I couldn't stand being told what to do; I couldn't see myself in a suit and tie; and that I had a vocation that precluded my getting settled into anything steady and reliable. This vocation was rather like the monster under one's bed, that forces one to leap from the light switch to the covers in order to avoid being caught by the ankles. Just as one forgets whether the monster is a bear or a monkey or a dragon, I had forgotten precisely what my vocation was going to be.

My anxiety not to be caught by a career caused me to be caught by all sorts of improbable jobs instead. At various times I swept leaves; weeded weeds; worked on cars; taught in South America; built shelves for bookshops; constructed stone walls and patios; and even contemplated working in a subterranean sewage plant that was carved into the cliffs near Brighton. I was put off by the paralysing stench and the depressed and wretched appearance of the strips of pink lavatory paper that were attached to the crushing wheel.

I confess that it was my desire to be a student again that caused me to do teacher-training, and I confess that I took my first teaching post simply because it was near to my girlfriend of the time. Later on I moved to London and worked as a supply teacher, because I had suddenly remembered that my vocation was to be a writer, and because the aforementioned girlfriend and her successor had both broken my heart by finding me wanting. Supply teachers do very little preparation or marking, and I was fully qualified for the job by virtue of my previous experience of being regularly assaulted and insulted by the nation's youth, and my former girlfriends.

Supply teachers have no control whatsoever over their destiny – they can be placed wherever an education authority capriciously or frivolously sees fit – and so it was that eventually I found myself working for three years in a truancy centre that I had helped to found simply by being there fortuitously at its inception.

It was a paradoxical concept, this school for school-refusers, and the astonishing thing about it was that we succeeded with about half of the pupils that we took on. Some came for one day, and then disappeared. Others came for a fortnight and then disappeared. Some we expelled for offences such as driving our cars away, or covering everything with tomato ketchup, or striking us with baseball bats. But we did manage to hold on to half of them, and I recently had the pleasure of being informed by one of our former pupils that he would have ended up in jail if not for us. 'It's early days,' I said, encouragingly, remembering that his neighbours had once accused him of molesting their little girl.

In my experience, school-refusers can be divided into two types. One is the incorrigibly anti-social maniac whose life is made impossible at school because they are always being told off and punished, and the other is the delicate flower (of either sex) that cannot stand the hurly-burly of school life. We were supposed to cater for both at once in the same institution, always bearing in mind the interesting variants of both types: the paranoid, the wildly humorous, the hair-trigger-tempered, the sex-obsessed, the victims of scabies and urticaria, the kleptomaniac, the cocky, the deliriously affectionate . . . What a lot of them had in common was a lonely mother who snatched at the slightest excuse to keep them at home, until they had lost so much education that they were ashamed to rejoin their classes. I only stopped working with them when I was sure that I could earn my living by writing, but I continued to go in every week to take sports with them, until eventually the centre closed. I used to say that I had a responsibility not to reject youngsters who had already suffered too much rejection, but I suppose the truth is that I had become too fond of them to leave them completely. On one of the Thursdays that I went in, we all decided to take a day out in Greenwich rather than caper about in the sports hall . . .

'Bloody 'ell, when are we going?' exclaimed Lyndsey, otherwise known as Mrs Catflap. She was fifteen years old, and was standing on a chair with her shorts around her knees while she adjusted the fit of her tights.

'Mind the gap,' I said, having adopted this exhortation as a means of discouraging her from such exhibitionism. 'Mind the gap' is normally heard on the Tannoy of the London Underground, as a caution to those who have to leap half a yard from train to platform, or vice versa.

'O fuck off, Louis,' she cried, and then added, 'I told my mum that you always say that.'

'Terrifying,' I replied. 'Tell your mum that if she comes here to beat me up, I'll set my cat on her.'

Mrs Catflap normally had beautiful copper hair, but today it was slime-green owing to an attempt to dye it black. She wriggled, pulled her shorts back up, and hopped off the chair. 'When are we bloody going?' she repeated.

'When Virge is off the phone.'

But Virge was seldom off the phone; it was her escape from the Truancy Centre. With the handpiece tucked against her cheek she would pluck at her split ends and light one cigarette after another, until there were two or three smouldering all at once in the ashtray, leaving delicately poised lengths of ash exactly nine centimetres long. The truants, to whom cigarettes were supremely precious, regarded this waste as a sacrilege.

'We're so busy,' she was saying, 'honestly, to tell you the absolute truth, we haven't had a moment, and we're completely rushed off our feet. To be quite honest with you, I'm absolutely up to my eyes.' It was the same conversation that Virge had with everyone on the phone, and it could last for hours. It was her method of blotting out the awful rigours of the little bedlam that we had created, but it had the effect of leaving the initiative to Tom and myself. Since I had officially left to be a writer, everything was in fact left to Tom. He was thought by the truants to resemble Winnie the Pooh, and so someone had pinned a notice above his chair that read 'Pooh Corner'. He always wore sandals, even in the rain, and filled his head and his files with details of every opera recording there had ever been. It was his enthusiasm and experience that kept the Truancy Centre going, and I had gratefully yielded the baton when Tom had arrived. He was a noisy and ebullient man, and therefore ideal for the job, whereas the Blessed Virge and I were washed out and brain-dead.

'When are we going?' asked Madeleine, otherwise known as Mrs Spongecake. She was fifteen, tall, blonde, lissom, tousled and sexually active. She would arrive in the morning fresh from the embraces of her boyfriend, immaculately made up, and would wrap herself languorously around any male that might offer her a cigarette. Once she had obtained one, she would abruptly and cynically break the embrace to go and smoke it at the bottom of the stairs.

While Virge talked, Mrs Spongecake smoked, Mrs Catflap adjusted her dress, and the boys played pool savagely in the next-door room, I went to unblock the girls' lavatory, which had filled to the brim because one of Mrs Catflap's sanitary towels had plugged the U-bend. I reflected on the manifold joys of teaching, and remembered that Virge had asked me to install a bog-roll dispenser. 'Please put your periodic offerings into the pedal bin provided,' I said to Mrs Catflap when I returned. 'It took four bucketfuls of water to get that one down the drain.'

Mrs Catflap, always genuinely horrified by any mention of periods, punched me hard, and I winced. Seeing my expression of pain, she said 'I love you really', and threw her arms around me. I patted her back in embarrassment, never really having known how to cope with affectionate adolescent pupils, and she drew back and slapped me in the face. 'Only joking,' she said, 'I really do love you really.' She reminded me of the kind of domestic cat that suddenly bites and scratches when overcome by pleasurable emotion. 'My dad says I've got feathers in my knickers,' she observed, and she danced over to the mirror to see whether or not her backside was too big. This involved teetering on tiptoe, and peering backwards over her shoulder.

Virge continued to talk about how busy she was, and outside in the pool-room Mitchell annoyed Anthony by asking him whether he had ever 'jooked' anybody. This was Battersea slang for stabbing. The reason that Mitchell asked this question was that Anthony was black, and Mitchell wanted to get in with him, since, like most young white boys, he wanted to participate in black youth culture; Mitchell had got the idea that black boys were interested in stabbing. Anthony, perceiving the racism in the enquiry, was outraged. 'What kind of stupid question is that?' he yelled, 'Get away from me, div. What do you think I am?' Mitchell retreated, and tried to think of some other way of impressing Anthony. He came into the staffroom and gazed longingly at Mrs Catflap's wonderful and perfect curves as exuberantly she tried to perform some high kicks. Tom was reading a book and holding out his hand for her to try and kick. She fell over backwards and lay on the floor, saying to no one in particular, 'O no, don't fucking laugh.' She saw that I was laughing, and got up. She pulled down her shorts, adjusted her tights, and I said 'Mind the gap' just before she hit me.

Wendy the secretary arrived, laden with black dustbin liners full of second-hand clothes from the market. She clothed everyone at the centre in raiment of her own flamboyant taste, all at knockdown prices. I had two drawers full of T-shirts, all sporting messages like 'Live Girls', and 'Stripped to kill', in which I used to work on my car during my spare time.

At last Virge put down the phone. It was now half past ten, and the intention had been to leave at half past nine. We waited for the boys to finish their game of pool, which they artificially prolonged for as long as possible, and finally everyone set off down the stairs, in the hope of sailing to Greenwich for the Centre's day out. Mrs Catflap was just saying to me, 'If you weren't so fucking old, fat, and bald, I could really fall in love with you, you've got such beautiful eyes,' when there was a crash, and shards of glass landed outside. Mitchell was trying to impress Anthony and the boys by vandalising the windows. His missiles were the school baked potatoes, which were so hard that they could have been used as anti-tank shells.

But he would not confess to it, and neither would the other

boys betray him. There occurred a convenient hiatus in proceedings because Virge had gone into the bank in order to get some money for the day out; she was in trouble because, in order to withdraw money, she needed Wendy the secretary's signature on the cheque as well as her own. She had forged it herself, and was now in difficulty with the cashier. Outside the bank, for an hour, Tom harangued the boys and I went to the bus-stop with the girls. Mrs Catflap ran between the two groups keeping everyone updated on the state of play, wide-eyed with delight at all the confrontation.

Tom told the boys that they could not come until someone owned up to smashing the window, just as Virge, flushed, emerged from the bank. Mrs Catflap relayed the news, adding, 'Frankie's slashed his wrists again. He's such a div.'

Frankie, enormously tall and rather overweight, slashed his wrists every time that he felt angry or frustrated, and was liable to do it with any conveniently sharp object in his immediate vicinity. He enjoyed the comfort and reassurance of having the wounds bandaged and plastered afterwards. I went over to him and said 'Scratch or cut?' and examined the bleeding wrists. I craned my neck upwards to look into Frankie's rubicund face, and told him severely, 'You really must find a better way of being angry,' whereupon Frankie nodded glumly in assent, and asked, 'Anyone got a plaster?' It turned out that nobody had.

Mitchell escaped from Tom, leaping on to the departing bus just as Virge, Nutty Roger, myself, and the girls were departing. Tom glared balefully from the street corner, having had his orders to the boys blatantly disobeyed. He returned to the Truancy Centre, leaving Virge and me entirely unaware of the fact that none of the boys were supposed to be with us, since no one had admitted to the smashing of the window.

At Sloane Square Virge went to a phone box and discovered that she had no change; she spent a quarter of an hour in various shops trying to obtain some, and then had a long conversation on the phone with Tom, who still furious. Meanwhile Frankie, his wrists dripping with blood, looking for all the world like a casualty of war, arrived on the next bus, and continued persistently to demand a plaster. Mrs Catflap kindly donated a slightly used tissue, and doe-eyed Lisa found another. Frankie sat on some steps contentedly whilst the girls fussed about him and called him a fucking loony. Mitchell resumed his ogling of Mrs Catflap's enviable assets, while Mrs Spongecake practised her wicked green eyes on me. When Virge reappeared it was nearly lunch-time, and she had resolved that we should all go to Hyde Park instead of Greenwich. Mrs Catflap chatted up a cheerful Chelsea Pensioner, resplendent in tricorn and scarlet tunic, who wanted to hang Mr Kinnock, the then Labour Party leader. The Blessed Virge took offence at this, and we all but missed a bus on account of the ensuing political discussion.

At Hyde Park the 'children' disappeared. Mitchell stole a can of soft drink from a refrigerator in the café, and shared it with Mrs Catflap, who by now was impressed with his abilities. Everybody suddenly realised that no one knew what had happened to Anthony; Virge went to a phone box, and I went to find the missing pupils. They were regrouped on the promise of a free ice-cream.

Frankie sullenly refused to go on a rowing boat, and spent the afternoon cruising about the Serpentine in the motorboat, his wrists still seeping blood into his tissues. The Blessed Virge, Nutty Roger and myself went in one rowing boat, uneventfully at first, and in another went doe-eyed Lisa, Mrs Spongecake, Mrs Catflap and Mitchell.

Virge and I watched in dismay as the other boat went round and round in circles, drifting away towards the far bridge. We observed the struggles of its crew with a mixture of alarm and amusement, and then Virge dropped an oar into the water, obliging me to stand up in the prow and paddle like an Indian to retrieve it. By the time that it was recovered, the other boat had disappeared without trace.

The rescue boat had to go out twice in order to find the lost rowing boat. They found it empty, with the oars missing, drifting like the *Marie Celeste* in the centre of the lake. Virge raised her eyes to the heavens and told me, 'Look, I've got a meeting to go to. Could you bring them all back? I can't wait any longer.' The Blessed Virge adored meetings with other teachers, because they consisted of long monologues in which we moaned in turn about the horrors of the job and the low level of pay.

She fled the scene of the fiasco and hailed a taxi, leaving me to bring home the diaspora of adolescents. I decided to go to the café, knowing that the kids would know that that was what I was doing, since, like all teachers, my unvarying response to a problem was to drink a cup of coffee and light up.

Doe-eyed Lisa and Mrs Spongecake appeared, informing me with breathless joy that they had given up trying to row the boat, and had just drifted about. The sunshine had worked its effect on Mitchell and Mrs Catflap, who were at this very moment somewhere in the rhododendrons, eating each other up and sighing with all the passion of unconsummated post-pubescence. While we waited, I had a water fight with Michelle, a sweet and amusing girl that I had not remembered bringing on the trip. Frankie, who fancied Mrs Catflap himself, went off to find her and Mitchell, consumed by a jealous rage that threatened to bring on some more wrist-mutilation.

No one returned. Michelle, Lisa, Mrs Spongecake, Nutty Roger and I wended our way to the bus-stop, and on the bus Mrs Spongecake draped her delicious body all over me, hugging me and kissing my neck as I wondered what to do about it. I felt that I should neither reject nor encourage her, and thus relying on my professional judgement, I let her sit happily on my knee like a little girl, all the way back to Battersea, while the others watched the scene with undisguised and somewhat anthropological interest. I sincerely wished that I had not been a teacher, and that I was seventeen years old, at which age beautiful young blondes had never seen fit to sit on my knee and attempt to seduce me. I also wished that I had no principles.

Back at the Truancy Centre it transpired that Anthony had doubled back and played pool on his own all day, Tom had gone home, Virge had disappeared to her meeting, and the school dinners had become welded to their plates in the warming trolley. I scraped all the food off and took it home to put on my compost heap, where it miraculously transformed itself overnight into a rank and heaving mass of maggots.

In the days that followed, Mrs Catflap and Mitchell continued to devour each other in public, and he cheerfully confessed to having broken the window in order to show off to the other boys. Nutty Roger broke another one by hurling another baked potato at it, thus establishing a firm tradition which continued unbroken until the day the centre was closed.

Mrs Catflap's romantic idyll continued until her sixteenth birthday, when Mitchell hopefully presented her with a packet of multicoloured and vari-flavoured condoms. She called him a dickhead, broke off the relationship, and, months later, her hair copper-coloured once again, she remained sad, wistful, and disillusioned. But her unhappiness had rendered her gentler; when she hugged me she no longer hit me immediately afterwards. She became as sombre and remote as the fourth symphony of Sibelius, grew anxious to please, and gave up calling everybody a fucking div.

The Blessed Virge swore that she would never take 'the kids' out again, and everyone was especially kind to Mrs Catflap, hoping that one day she would again get feathers in her knickers. Even a trip to Chessington Zoo a while later failed to restore them, however, and Mitchell, unable to cope with Mrs Catflap's rejection, thenceforward truanted permanently from the Truancy Centre.

People often ask me if I miss teaching. I certainly don't miss the anxiety of teetering at the edge of a relentlessly crumbling precipice, but I do miss some of my pupils. They gave me my best jokes and an undying sense of the absurd, and some of them gave me so much affection and loyalty and amusement that I will never feel unloved again. Some of them write to me, often with touching and rather shocking frankness, and I meet others on the street who have transformed themselves from hopeless cases into engineers and accountants, hairdressers and mechanics. All the boys are a foot taller than me, and can't stop themselves from addressing me as 'sir' when we meet in the street. Strangers ask me whether or not I have children, and this always makes me smile. I've got hundreds and hundreds of them. One or two of them attacked me with chairs and knives and bottles, and most of them were outright in their verbal abuse. But there were many that I will always remember and always miss, even though almost every day was like the one that I have just described. I feel rather like the explorer who is glad it's over, but glad he did it, with wounds that don't hurt any more, and many tales to tell.

Drinking Maté

Reuben Lane

THERE WAS A photo in the album of me between my mum and dad. I cut it out with a sharp Stanley knife. A boy in grey flannel shorts and white Airtex shirt.

I put him in the sky – in an aeroplane – in a leather helmet and goggles.

I put him on a stage – huge breasts squeezed – the heroine standing belting to the Gods.

I put him in a convent in a wimple and high heels.

I put him out of reach of all the mothers waiting outside the playground gates in their cars at a quarter to four.

I'm like the figures my sister used to buy Saturdays from WH Smith's – cut out and stand – dress them up – party; beach; school.

I rang the bell. A little old lady with an arched back stood staring up at me. One eye bigger than the other. There was a smell inside of toilet fluid and fried potatoes.

I showed her the boy in the cut-out photo.

'Have you seen him – is he hiding here?'

She cupped the picture in her hand and rocked him like Tom Thumb. She pointed to her mouth. Her lips were stitched with garden twine. Her eyes said 'Let me out'.

Inside – I pushed through – and the walls began to crumble and the little old woman hid beneath a huge jam pan.

And the roof collapsed. And the sky was full of faces. Big wide-beamed smiles. Cemetery headstones. And they sang. And ladders fell to the ground – to rescue me up. As I climbed – the rungs started snapping.

111

Garcia drives to my house. I'm in the passenger seat. Highbury roundabout. Canonbury. Over Essex Road. Old Street. And after the lights past the London Apprentice. He says: 'I never realised that was there.' Although it's a place he used to visit with Rod – and we pass this way once or twice a week. He says: 'But I keep my eyes on the road.' And it makes me wonder, as I navigate us through London, what's going on inside his head – if he isn't like me observing outside – mapping it down? Each time somewhere completely else – the two of us in the same car – on very different trips.

Last night – after we'd seen a film at the Gay Film Festival – we sat in the bar. And Garcia explained why he chooses to keep his sexuality a secret; from people at work; from his mum and dad; from certain friends. He said 'It's like drugs – people have all these ideas – what type of people take drugs – what sort of people are gay. And I don't want them to think that about me. I don't want their shit. It's my business – it's got nothing to do with them.' I said taking drugs and being gay were completely different issues. He said my attitude was very young. And he raised his voice – wriggling about – changing directions. Surrounded by hundreds of lesbians and gay men – my boyfriend, in a loud voice – lambasting me for being openly gay.

And suddenly I yelled at him, 'I'm not going to be one who keeps his mouth, or his sexuality, zipped up tight for safety's sake or the comfortable life.'

Kew Bridge. 6.15 Friday evening. Along – under it – the coots and the mallards. Flame-orange lights throwing long undamaged lines out over the water. The trail by the side of the Thames squelchy. A soft drizzle. And I want to give it all away. All my goings on. I want to be on my own so I can walk beside this river all night. Like the lone rower who cuts the water with his oars. A baseball cap and a red KitKat sweatshirt. He waves – I wave back. No one else around. The motor launches moored – bedtime – at the water's edge. The glass houses in Kew Gardens. The six tower blocks on the north side. Barking geese. Nothing missing. A hazy day slips down the river with the London junk. Heathrow planes – fin lights blinking. And I realise other people's troubles are not my own.

Told from the roof of the cinema.

The silver dome of the mosque. TV aerials and chimney-pots. Hospital helicopters. The revolving amber light on the corner; DRIVERS WANTED. To Let Shop Unit with Restaurant consent, Carpet Corner, Betterspecs, Betty's Card and Gift Centre. The halal butchers. The electricity pylons and construction cranes, tower blocks, everywhere on the horizon – three hundred and sixty degrees. Ganesha – the Hindu god with the head of an elephant.

Children's skin bulging with Easter chocolate. White plastic bags – lost balloons tossed and scuttering along the blotchy pavement.

I must go down – no watch on my wrist – no public clock in sight – out here in Dalston where time doesn't matter – the High Street busy day or night. The aluminium ladder rail. Falling on to the top of a red double-decker bus. Thump. 'What was that?' The passengers inside. An angel on the roof, hitching a free ride.

The caw of a blackbird. The green fake grass over the stacked milk crates outside the Turkish supermarket dancing in the whisper of the wind. Boxes of still oranges and knobbly roots of ginger. Satellite dishes. Church spires with Gothic bumps. Rainbow swings and astro turf.

Last night – did you see it? – a total lunar eclipse. Garcia had heard about it on the radio. He woke up one of his housemates – and we piled into her room – five of us lying on the floor – lights off – looking out through the open window – the moon moving across the sky. We shifted every few minutes so we could all see. At first, a tiny smudge on the rim. And over the course of an hour a circle of charcoal slid across the white. And Garcia said, 'Look – it's red – the moon's going red – they say it's blood – and when the moon is totally immersed in the cone of darkness they say it loses all its power.' We looked – but the eclipse was grey. Until the last meniscus vanished, and suddenly a raspberry colour spread over the darkened moon.

We opened a bottle of Argentinian red wine and toasted the eclipse.

All evening Garcia kept hugging me. 'Oh hon – I really love you,' kissing me in front of everyone. And I – strange me – just said, 'Oh, that's nice'.

Upstairs in his room he tried to explain to me the astronomy of an eclipse. Outside the moon was darkening over in a second cone. He told me the Chinese say that the moon is like a dragon, as it journeys the sky it rides up and down.

We laid his mattress in the bay of the window so we could watch as the eclipse waned. And Garcia fucked me. Pushing into me again and again.

He said, 'Look – the moon.' And there – blinding – the milky edge returning.

We both came. And we held fast to each other – my knees on his chest – before he pulled out of me – a sticky squelch as he knotted the end of the condom. Hunting in his laundry basket for a dirty T-shirt to mop us dry.

'Are you sleeping, hon – or are you watching?'

Stacked against each other. The soft pillow.

'Both,' I murmur. The power returning to the moon.

I went out looking for bits of me. And this is who I found.

A man with a rolled-up mattress trudging the platform of the Underground.

An usherette at the back of the cinema shining the torch down – beaming the hem of her skirt and her scuffed black shoes.

A man in a tan cowboy hat – sitting second row from the front – flicking his wrist – rattling his gold plaited bracelet.

The janitor at the swimming pool, standing at the edge when all the people have gone, leaning on the end of his mop, the other end wedged into a metal pail of disinfectant. Listening to the sound of emptiness; children shouting, water splashing, the yells of the lifeguard: 'Oi – don't run' – sunken to the bottom of the sky-blue pool.

A tired white businessman sitting at the wheel of his car –

waiting for the Nigerian men in their navy overalls and yellow boots to soap and wash the chrome. There are two signs he stares at as he loosens his tie and undoes his shirt collar button; one is a picture of a cigarette with a red line through it. The other asks, 'Are all your windows shut?'

A woman with a blonde rinse and swollen ankles who steps off the edge of the escalator and looks back a moment – the metal grooves of each step eaten up, the rubber handbelt spooling back.

The girl at the hairdressers restacking on the glass coffee table a pile of *Hello!* and *She* magazines. Sweeping up strands of lost hair – a panful of ginger and brunette.

And the bald-headed man – unlocking the frosted glass door to his block of flats – muttering under his breath: 'No you don't. No you don't.'

Two days of little worries. To and from the housing benefit office in Greatorex Street. Not understanding why my benefit's been suspended – scanning their letters – trying to make sense of it. The young Glaswegian woman behind the desk, swinging her ponytail: 'It's the computer. We can't interfere with it.' Filling out the application form again – trying to remember what I put last time. The man behind with three forms from the Salvation Army hostel on Whitechapel High Street. A veiled Muslim woman talking on the phone to the office upstairs.

I end up saying things – doing things – being the sort of person I used to steer clear of.

The morning of Garcia's birthday. He goes to early zazen. It's raining. I cycle half a mile to a café in Stoke Newington for a peppermint tea and a croissant, sitting at a table in the window upstairs, top deck of the double-deckers level with me – the passengers behind the steamed-up glass – we catch each others' eyes. And I wonder what else I should buy Garcia for his birthday – a kite and a bunch of flowers?

I told Garcia I'd give him some of the cells from my brain – my organisational skills. And he said – folded close together – Yes – but what if you gave me the cells that has you throwing eggs, shouting and hitting me? I said the surgeon was already on his way.

A fair blue sky – an aeroplane scudding a trail of ice crystals.

I complicate. I mesmerise.

A refrigerator rusting on the iron steps – waiting to be handled off to the dump.

A flurry of pigeons. And my worries lift off – swoop down and glide up over the rooftops.

I walked along the street. Chosen – a limousine pulled up. A woman wound down the window.

'Hi,' she said. 'Wanna lift?'

'I'm not going anywhere.' I said.

'Neither am I,' she said. 'Hop in.'

And inside the back of the limousine was a mini-bar, a TV set and a bucket of ice. She sat beside me.

'Excuse me.'

She dipped a hand into the bucket and rubbed an ice cube under her armpits. And then she popped the cube into her mouth and crunched it with her teeth.

Last night we went to an Amnesty International meeting about the Dirty War in Argentina, when an estimated 30,000 dissidents were 'disappeared' by the military junta.

Garcia was a student the last couple of years, and he went with a group from college to the street demonstrations. He said they were very organised – everyone's name was taken and checked at the end of the demo. They would link arms forming a circle if there was any trouble. The police mounted on horseback with batons and riot shields. At the time he would argue with his father: 'Look what's happening.' And his father would tell him his Leftie friends were putting ideas in his head. After 1984 when the truth started to filter out – the mass graves, the mothers and grandmothers marching outside the Casa Rosada around the obelisk demanding to know, holding up photos of their missing children – his father admitted that he'd been wrong. The fates of the disappeared remain locked away in the Army files.

And Garcia couldn't get to sleep, fretting – his job, his

country, his parents – never making any firm decisions, 'like a teenager'. And all I can do when he's like this is hug him – press us as close together as possible – tell him – idiotically repetitive: 'I love you.'

This morning – one of the few mornings Garcia stays over at mine – we wake up late, and he has to tumble down the stairs to feed the parking meter (20p for eight minutes). He buys some bagels from the bakery while I make us a coffee and tuck the bed sheets back in.

In Soho Square the council men change the black sacks, stretching them across the mouths of each bin, whilst others rake the soil and roll out layers of fresh turf – a luxury green – for all the gorgeous people to decorate this next summer heatwave.

I go and have a pot of tea and a raisin pastry in the top room of Maison Bertaux – sugary almond paste in the middle. The windows are open and cigarette smoke is sucked outside; sunlight rests on the net curtains tied up with aquamarine ribbon. A faded fifties colour photo framed on the wall – Mont St Michel. The proprietress carries a three-month-old baby on one arm, tonging cakes from the glass shelves with her free hand. Two American leather guys talk about 'The Straights' whilst eating *tarte citron*.

And me: I feel as if someone has planted the palms of their hands on the sternum of my ribcage and they're pressing down on me – push a fraction harder and I'll break into tears.

So I go back to Soho Square – where the sun has slipped. Everyone spoons yoghurt or munches sandwiches; the cycle couriers swig from giant bottles of lemonade. Feathers and plane tree fluff caught between the pavement cracks.

With Garcia I burst through a hundred emotions – but the loudest, the clearest, the most compelling – is always anger. And with every fight we have, part of me breathes a sigh of relief – that this is it, at last – the inevitable goodbye.

The scent of pale yellow and thick maroon primulas. A fat couple wobble with laughter. And I grow nostalgic for the days when I was on my own and feeling sad, I'd go out – walk myself tired – feel the moment my sadness lifted – and carry myself home – safe – my sole dependent.

A blonde-haired woman carrying a pot of basil heading down to Frith Street smiles at me as if we've met somewhere before.

I spent this morning cold – wrapped up in bed. But it's better, out, with plenty of places for my fury to float away; get left behind; a tea cup at Maison Bertaux; a strand of hair; a flake of skin dropped beneath this bench.

Dungeness. We got up at the crack of dawn; tube to Victoria; the train to Ashford 'International'.

We caught a bus to Lydd. Coffee and sweet cherry shortbread in a bakery there. 'To Dungeness and the sea' on the signpost. Garcia asked at the bakery to fill our thermos up with hot water. We walked along the edge of the road. Followed a sign to a bird sanctuary – binoculars trained on the salt marshes. The old ladies at the desk didn't know where Derek Jarman's garden was. We crossed a moon landscape – the fifties nuclear reactor like a white palace, terrifying in its hugeness and remoteness in the mist. We came to a fence – slid underneath it – a tarmac road that led to the power station.

We eventually got to Dungeness. The foghorn and the lamp in the lighthouse going. We stopped in the lifeboat house – Garcia bought a postcard and a romantic adventure for his mum. The big man, who used to be captain on board before he got too old, now in charge of the souvenirs shop, pointed along the shingle shore to a black pitched house with a yellow door: 'That's where the garden is.' We went first and sat by the sea – fishing skiffs hauled high and dry – ate some rye bread and cheese – and I rolled a joint in the wind. Garcia unscrewed a jam jar, shook some dry green yerba leaves out into the maté cup and filled it to the brim with hot water. We took it in turns sucking the drink up through a tin straw (the bombillia) and refilling from the thermos. The very bitter taste at the beginning began to gentle as the cup journeyed from his mouth to mine and back again.

Then the garden – no fence around it – you can go right up to the back door – '*Entrée des artistes*' – spirals and patterns of stones, driftwood, old buoys – objects found on the beach – holed pebbles and shells strung on iron forks. On the side of the house – a poem written in leather letters. Garcia lay on the ground angling his camera. I could see Derek Jarman wandering through his garden – gently stirring the pebbles.

I sit on a leather padded bench in the British Library. Next to a marble bust of Dr Charles Burney. And through a glass cabinet – the Christian Orient – I recognise the black-suited figure loping like a bear coming this way. It's my uncle. And I dip my head and doodle in the margin. He comes and sits down at the other end of the bench. We catch each other's glance – his face angry. And he barely sits half a minute before slouching into the next room. What is it about me that scares him, that can't even bring him to mouth 'Hello'? I once went up to him in the bar of a theatre and said, 'I'm your nephew.' And he said, 'I know,' and walked away.

Last night Garcia and I rowed so loud the new people in the flat below banged a broom-handle against the ceiling.

And I'm sorry for throwing your things around – for tipping your plants on the floor – for thumping you. The ashes of your stripey socks. Burnt rubber. Climbing the lip of the barricades. And you tell your friends: 'He's a lunatic – a fucking lunatic.'

I went to visit Valerie in Brixton. Her flat on Effra Road which she shares with her best friend Pete. The rooms immaculate – stripped and polished floorboards, peppermint green skirting and window frames. The flat had belonged to a man who had died of Aids and when Valerie moved in there was a collection of rocks and stones along the window-sill. Pete had wanted to throw them out. But Valerie has kept them there – adding to their number after trips to the seaside.

She says she's going through a strange phase in her life. And I say I'm always going through a strange phase. Then I think to myself – shut up and listen. We're having pizzas out in the Brixton Market arcade. Across the way – weird fish in polystyrene boxes – the fishmongers in white nylon coats and blue wellington boots. And all the time drifting into us the couple at the next table are talking about what movies they've seen. Valerie doesn't know what's coming next – biding her time while Pete's paperwork goes through and the both of them move back to Australia in the winter. She looks forward to the summer and being able to walk to the lido in Brockwell Park – although this year she'll have to keep covered up in Chinese silk – the melanoma tissue they cut out of her last September.

And I'm remembering the last time I sat at one of these tables outside Franco's Pizzeria – two summers ago, with Denny – and how he too was talking about going to Australia. How he'd finish his novel in Sydney, and how he was feeling down about what his agent had told him, and how the flat he shares with his boyfriend was in a mess and his boyfriend was coming home from New York the next day. So I went back with him and got through a kitchenful of washing up while Denny hoovered the sitting-room and took a bath. And somehow we'd ended up together on the bed talking – and just as we'd about stopped talking and were going to strip out of our clothes – the telephone rang and it was Denny's boyfriend saying what time the plane was flying in. And I'd realised it was time I went or I'd be late for work.

Valerie finished her glass of *caffè latte*. And she showed me a new second-hand bookshop along Coldharbour Lane. I found a book of Lorrie Moore's stories and bought it for Valerie because she reminds me of her. And I realise from the photo on the back cover they look quite like each other – although Valerie would laugh if she heard me say it. And Valerie kisses me goodbye and says, 'Sorry if I've been a bit lacking in energy today.' And I say she hasn't – it's been fun. And I meant to tell her, the whole time I was with her, she's looking really good, but I forgot and I felt annoyed with myself when I remembered again – cycling along Kennington Road.

Retrospective

Elizabeth Kay

YOU MIGHT SAY I was lucky to have a job at all, but I don't think luck comes into it. White males under thirty with the right background are in short supply these days – children are just too expensive for the educated classes. The underclass breed like rabbits, of course.

From my window I could see the polystyrene shacks on the green, and I could watch the clogs trying to bum new ecus off the passers-by. I don't know when we started to to call them clogs. It was a sort of word-play on the dispossessed – those who inhabit the crumbly white periphery of our towns and villages, the peasants who might have worn clogs in a bygone age, the human detritus that clogs the machinery of our cities. London has been clogged to the eyeballs for decades. Personally, I try not to look.

The only reason I was watching that morning was because the new computer had arrived, and the manual took up three whole bookshelves. I decided not to rush it, poured myself another cup of inka and watched the leaves fall off the sycamore tree. It was, as you have probably guessed, the rainy season. They used to call it autumn in gentler times, before the hurricanes made wind tunnels between the tower blocks and the rain was acid enough to eat into the architecture as well as the foliage.

My eyes were caught by a particularly spectacular leaf, red and gold and curled at the edges. It reminded me of something I'd seen in the Tate – *Crumpled Fag Packet in Suspension* – by someone whose name escapes me, so I watched as it

123

descended in a leisurely spiral until it landed on the grass. Two clogs were struggling with one another nearby – a not uncommon sight; what *was* unusual was the knife that appeared as if from nowhere and the way that the silver blade turned suddenly and unexpectedly as red as my leaf.

The taller of the two scrambled to his feet and ran, clutching a sheaf of papers and a handful of credit cards. His image remained etched on my retina as clearly as if I'd photographed him. A pair of quilted boots, black with a dragon or a serpent or something embossed on the heels, and one of those long dark cloaks they all wear. I caught a fleeting glimpse of carrot-red dreadlocks and then he was gone. The other one just lay there, the way so many of them do when there's been an especially hard frost. I kept expecting someone to come and do something, another clog, the militia perhaps, a passer-by even, although that was unlikely. No one came. In the end I had to go down myself, although it occurred to me later that I could have rung the authorities from where I was.

I didn't *want* to go down there, of course. No one really wants to mix with the clogs because they're always hassling you for something, your gloves or some bread or a spare contraceptive. It's a bit like bolting the stable door after the horse has gone – most of them are going to die from exposure or starvation or disease anyway. You just don't want them to do it on your doorstep.

It took me a good fifteen minutes to get down as the lift was broken again. Naturally I was hoping that the problem would have got up and walked away by the time I got there, but life isn't like that.

The clog was male, thirty-ish, and bleeding profusely. I didn't touch him. I merely told him that I was going to call an ambulance, although we both knew that the likelihood of it reaching him in time was remote. If you've got the right policy you can get a heli-ambulance. The other sort take hours.

He whispered something that sounded remarkably like 'I'm insured', which had to be a lie. Clogs can't afford insurance.

'Come again?' I said, although I didn't bend any closer.

'Insured,' he hissed. 'Number's in my pocket.'

He must have realised that I wasn't going to look because he started to fumble with his coat – it had some sort of inside pocket – and that's when the letter fell out. I saw his eyes drift towards it.

'I'm going to telephone right now,' I said. I mean, I didn't want him lying there, not directly beneath my window.

He didn't reply, and all of a sudden there was something not quite right about his face. I just stood there. I knew he was dead, and I suppose I was wondering how I ought to feel. I didn't arrive at any conclusions, so after a little while I went back upstairs and phoned for the ambulance. For some inexplicable reason I took the letter with me.

There's always money for advances in computer technology, even if there isn't any money for anything else. The new one was called Jennifer, for reasons that were never made clear to me. She was a beautiful little creation, all metallic green with the very latest in hologramatic animation. The most important thing, however, was the fact that she could think for herself. She could actually write her own programs, once you told her what the problem was. The only problems she was likely to encounter in our office were interpersonal ones, and I doubted whether she had the appropriate skills to deal with those.

We humans deal with investments here. Buying and selling really modern works of art, and making a tidy profit in the process. We've got quite a few of the big names – Tadeusz Twardowski, who paints with body fluids; Roland Spickett, the one who uses microscopes and bacteria; and Donald Barnes. Donald Barnes was the really big money-spinner with his series on toenail clippings, and the fact that he'd died of a heart attack the previous week had made him worth considerably more. Cranford Smith (my employer) always held back plenty of pieces in the warehouse so that he could make a killing after a death. Sound economic sense, really. All his artists had to agree to it, and also not to store more than a certain number of works themselves – it would never do for the relatives to flood the market straight after the funeral. Cranford would let the pieces appear gradually, so that the price never suffered. The man had made a fortune, which was why he could afford to indulge in his other little interest, computers. We didn't really *need* Jennifer, although there were obvious advantages to some of her applications. The hologramatic representations were going to be very useful for showing clients large sculptural pieces, particularly if they hadn't actually been constructed. You could make a maquette look twenty times its real size and site it straddled across the Thames if you chose to.

I loaded up *Toenail Clipping number 43 with London Clay* to see what it looked like. It was a remarkably faithful portrayal, with the little twist at the end of the clipping smeared with grey. The Third World ones have sold the best, with the one encrusted with oil-soaked sand fetching a quarter of a million. 'This tragic reconstruction of human debris is a powerful comment on the sharp practice employed by the shoe industry in under-developed countries', was what one leading newspaper had said, and although a rival paper had come back with 'Donald ducks the issue', the first observation stuck. Donald became known as an extremely serious exponent of the New Organic School of painting, and his prices rocketed.

I never quite knew how seriously Cranford viewed his work, however. Sincerity wasn't Cranford's strongest suit, although he was very well regarded by the critics and regularly appeared on *Spot The Forgery*. He had all the right phrases on the tip of his tongue and that's half the battle, isn't it, whatever field you're in.

I was just loading up another piece when Cranford breezed into the office. 'Good morning, minion,' he threw at me on his way past. 'What's new? Apart from Jennifer, of course.'

'There's been a murder,' I said, and that stopped him in his tracks.

'It's not anyone on our books is it?'

'A clog,' I told him, 'right under our window.'

'Oh.'

'I called an ambulance.'

'Mm.'

'He died right in front of me, while I was talking to him.'

Cranford wrinkled his upper lip in an expression of distaste.

'He said he was insured.'

'You're kidding.'

'Straight up,' I said, glad to have caught his interest for once. 'Oh,' I added, suddenly remembering, 'he had a letter . . .' I took it out of my pocket and looked at it for the first time. It was addressed to a Mr Smith, but the destination was obscured with something that looked like blood. 'Christ,' I said, leaping to my feet, 'I'd better wash my hands.'

Cranford was still wearing gloves. 'Give it to me,' he said, 'I'll bin it.' He glanced at the envelope. 'Smith? It might be for me.'

I snorted. 'That's not very likely is it,' I told him, 'not from a clog. Anyway, there are thousands of Smiths.'

He glared at me. I've never worked out why he didn't change his surname as well as his forename. Cranford was a considerable improvement on Fred, but why stop there? I don't really understand the man at all, but he makes a lot of money, and given enough time I'll work out exactly how he does it. Then I can branch out on my own.

I was very busy for the rest of the day, sorting things out for Donald Barnes's retrospective. When I popped my head round the door to say good night to Cranford he appeared a little distracted, which was unusual, and I noticed the clog's letter on his desk. 'Anything of interest?' I asked.

'What? Oh, no. You were right. Wrong Smith.' Cranford screwed the letter up into a little ball and threw it into the shredder. The shredder wasn't working again but I wasn't going to tell him, not when I was on my way home.

Of course, the first thing I had to do the next morning was repair the shredder, and so I had to remove all the rubbish Cranford had chucked in there the previous day. I suppose it was Cranford's unease the night before that made me smooth out the sheet of paper and read what was written on it. It wasn't such a strange thing to do, because I often read Cranford's private mail. I was building up a dossier of artists I would approach when the time was right to strike out alone.

There was no address at the top of the page, nor any polite preamble. It simply said: *It may interest you to know that Donald Barnes kept a large proportion of his work at a secret address, contrary to the terms of his agreement with you. I know the location, and you can expect to hear from me again when you have had sufficient time to mull over the implications. Rex.*

Not the wrong Smith at all, then. I could smell money here, lots of it, enough to set up an agency. I repaired the shredder, but I kept the letter.

The militia aren't terribly interested in clog murders – there's no money in them. That was why I was surprised to receive a visit from them later in the day, and even more surprised to learn that the corpse hadn't been a clog at all.

'He *looked* like a clog,' I said, 'scrawny. Who was he?'

'Enzo Andretti. You didn't see anything?'

'No.'

'He had some connections with a gallery in Bond Street, that's why we thought we'd try up here. You've never heard of him?'

'No.'

'Seems like a fairly straightforward mug. No money left on him, no plastic either. Just his hospital insurance number.'

'Oh,' I said, mentally listing the galleries on Bond Street. Cranford had called in sick, so they didn't speak to him, which also meant that I was able to take the rest of the day off – once I'd programmed Jennifer to take any phone calls and to finish cataloguing The Toenail Series.

I started at Fernando's. 'We've already had the militia round,' said the girl at reception, bored, 'and I told them just what I'm telling you. Enzo was a scout. Went round the art schools, minor exhibitions, that sort of thing. I don't think we ever took him up on any of his finds. Too traditional. Comes from having an upbringing steeped in Botticelli and Caravaggio I suppose. Here's his card. He always left one, we've got dozens.' She spotted a potential customer admiring a piece by Stirling. It was called *Requiem in Bile* and it was expensive. The boredom vanished in a flash as she homed in, all synthetic fibres and florescent colours, so I left. I'd got Enzo's address, and that was all that mattered.

It was one of those little box affairs they used to call 'starter homes', built to last to the end of the guarantees and no longer. The guarantees had run out many times over by now, and the laminates were peeling away like layers of skin, revealing the tubercular structure beneath. The only vote of confidence in the house had been the new front door – mild steel with mortice locks and shipping bolts. Most of the other boxes had them as well. The ones that didn't obviously didn't have anything worth nicking, and you could see right inside one living-room through a hole in the wall. There was no reply when I knocked at number twenty-four, but a small girl appeared almost instantaneously from number twenty-two. ' 'E ain't in,' she said with obvious relish, ' 'e's bin murdered.'

'Didn't he live with anyone?' I asked, resisting a strong impulse to bat the child round the ear.

'Nah, 'e was foreign.'

'Foreigners don't all live on their own,' I said, irritated, 'otherwise they'd die out, wouldn't they?'

She looked at me as though I'd spoken in Urdu. After a moment or two she suddenly said: 'She went back.'

'Who did?'

'Got any ecus?'

'They're called new ecus since the crisis.' I gave her a couple. There was, after all, a chance that they might turn into a sound investment.

''Is missus. Mrs Andretti. But she's coming back for the funeral, next week.'

'Tuesday? Wednesday?'

'Thursday.'

It was a pity, but there it was. I would have to pursue another line of inquiry for the next few days.

I phoned in sick the next morning. 'I must have caught your bug,' I told Cranford, who was hardly likely to deny the possibility, impossible as it was. 'You don't suppose Roland Spickett's moved on to viruses instead of bacteria, do you . . .?'

'I'll see you tomorrow,' Cranford said shortly, 'it only lasts twenty-four hours.'

I wondered what line of inquiry he'd been pursuing the previous day. Donald Barnes's family was a good each-way bet. It wouldn't do for me to descend on them as well *just* yet, it would be better to start ferreting around among the clogs. I didn't like the idea but it had to be done.

✳

It was a surprisingly still morning for October. There was one of those acidic mists hanging about that made you take your pollution mask just in case. I kept it hidden because clogs can't afford masks, and I was going to have to pretend to be one. I got myself a set of clothes at a second-hand shop. I believe they were once called charity shops for a while, until people stopped giving them their cast-offs and started selling them again, just like they used to.

I wore a pair of jeans and a duffle coat. I didn't shave, and I blackened my nails with some earth from a potted plant. There wasn't much I could do about the slight paunch I've developed recently, but after all, anyone can become a clog, all you have to do is to make a few wrong decisions and there's your expensive education down the plug hole.

I started with the shacks in Priory Park, because I didn't want Cranford glancing out of the window and spotting me. The clogs had got a fire going in the middle of the old fountain – there's never been any water in it during my lifetime – and it worked rather well, blazing up out of a giant stone shell and illuminating the cherub that was trying in vain to quench it with part of its anatomy. There was a group of them sitting round it, sharing a cigarette and coughing every so often in a companionable sort of way. I hovered for a while until one of them noticed me.

'You're new, aren't you.'

I nodded.

'Made redundant?'

I nodded again.

'You actually had a *job?*' The clog pushed back its hood, and I realised that I was talking to a girl.

'I'm looking for someone,' I said nervously.

'Oh?' said the girl. 'Twenty new ecus.'

'Eh?'

'All right, fifteen.'

'You don't understand,' I said, 'I'm looking for a particular *person*. He's got black quilted boots with a dragon or something on them, orangey hair, quite tall . . .'

She shook her head. 'Sorry.'

I got up.

'I could ask around.'

I waited for her to tell me how much *that* would cost but instead a dreamy look came over her face and she said, 'I bet you've had a bank account and everything. Who did you use to work for?'

'An agency.'

'Selling what?'

'Art.'

'*Wow.*'

'It wasn't *that* great.'

'I love paintings. Little windows into the past. That *Supper at Emmaus*, by Caravaggio. You can see exactly what they were eating.'

'What *who* were eating? The disciples or seventeenth-century Italians?' I was getting sick to death of Caravaggio.

'Cotman, then. He did some beautiful watercolours.'

Watercolours? How *outré* can you get? 'I'm a convinced modernist,' I said. 'The need for representationalism vanished with the invention of the camera. Art is now free to address itself directly to the subconscious, once you dispense with the formal visual language.'

To my surprise she didn't ask me to translate what I'd just said into English. Instead she said: 'So you like Donald Barnes and people like that.'

I felt myself stiffen. 'Why choose Donald Barnes as an example?'

'Rex use to work for him, gardening I think.'

'Rex?' I tried to sound reasonably off-hand.

'One of the guys.'

'Is he here? Can I speak to him?'

'I haven't seen him for a week or two, but I expect he'll be back.'

'Why did he stop working for Donald Barnes?'

'He probably got the sack. He's a bit unreliable. Why are you so interested?'

I tried to soft-pedal for a bit. 'He's very famous, Donald Barnes. And I'm a great admirer of his work, actually.'

'Toenail clippings?'

'They're very profound pieces. Everyone has toenails, they just don't pay much attention to them.'

The girl began to giggle.

'The symbolism can get a bit complicated,' I said, 'you really need a good grounding in everything from Conceptualism to the New Organic School . . . What's the matter?'

'The New Organic School?' She laughed outright this time. 'Sounds like an agricultural college. Oh, honestly, you can't take that stuff seriously, surely?'

'Certainly I do,' I said. 'It represents contemporary thought.'

The girl smiled. 'You're right there. Contemporary thought advocates taking as many people for a ride as possible.'

I got up.

'You're not a clog at all, are you?' she said suddenly. 'Nor was that Enzo Andretti Rex was with last week.'

Enzo and Rex? Curiouser and curiouser. 'Enzo is dead,' I told her, 'and I'm going to find the person who killed him.'

I thought it sounded great. She didn't seem terribly impressed. Maybe she'd never seen any John Wayne films. After all, she was only a clog.

I didn't really want to go to work the next day, but I couldn't see any alternative. Cranford was in a bad mood, and left shortly after I arrived. This gave me plenty of opportunity to program Jennifer to do all the work whilst I sat and deduced. By mid-morning all I'd deduced was that I was no good at deduction. Jennifer had finished all the cataloguing in a tenth of the time it took me to do it, and was twiddling her microprocessor thumbs. I was drinking my fifth cup of inka and watching the sycamore leaves when it suddenly occurred to me that I could feed all the information to Jennifer and see what *she* made of it.

'Well,' said Jennifer, in her slightly irritating real-person style, 'one scenario is that whilst Rex was working for Donald Barnes he found out that his employer was contravening the terms of his contract by hoarding his own work. Rex found out *where* Barnes was storing it, and decided to use Enzo as a middle man to approach Cranford, so that he didn't get ripped off. I expect they'd agreed a percentage.'

'So where does the killer with the ginger dreadlocks come in?'

'Not enough data,' said Jennifer.

'You said that was *one* scenario.'

'Figure of speech.'

'Computers aren't meant to have figures of speech,' I told her. 'I wonder what these paintings are like. Are they a completely different series? What was Barnes going to do with them? Had he completed them? Who's entitled to them now that he's dead?'

'Cranford is,' said Jennifer, and she went into hologram mode. I watched, fascinated.

First of all she created a huge white canvas against the wall. Then she painted it matt purple, fading from a deep alizarin violet at one end to a pale lilac at the other. After that she sketched in some squiggles and coloured them a deep glossy brown, so that the light caught them differently as you moved round. The final touch was a light sprinkling of white on the apex of one of the curves. It was breathtaking, and it could so easily have been a Donald Barnes.

'*Pubic Hair number 13 with dusting powder*,' said Jennifer, 'or something like that.' She wiped it and did another. This one was a single eyelash with a touch of blue mascara at one end.

'Where have you seen these, Jennifer?' I asked.

'I haven't. I made them up.'

'You what?'

'I made them up. I know what all the other Donald Barnes paintings look like. He's easy. Caravaggio's a lot more difficult because you have to spend a long time on the composition.'

'You can *draw*?'

'Well, I wouldn't call doing a Donald Barnes exactly *drawing* . . . more a bit of a doodle, really.'

'You don't rate him very highly, do you.'

'I don't rate him at all. Art's meant to be visual. He has to explain his paintings with pretentious titles and long discourses in esoteric magazines, so he doesn't count.'

'He counts in the art world.'

133

'You mean the world of investments. That's not the art world. The art world is in front rooms and on kitchen walls. It isn't who it's by, it's what it's like. If you can't tell the difference between a Canaletto and a fake there is no difference.'

'Try telling that to Cranford,' I said, smiling, 'he's on *Spot The Forgery* again next week.'

'Cranford knows it already,' said Jennifer. 'He's only in this business for the money. But you believe all the propaganda, don't you?'

And because I couldn't accuse Jennifer of having an angle I started to think about it.

At the weekend I returned to the park. The girl was still there, thin and pale and drowning in clothes that were too big for her. This time I took a loaf of bread and some sausage, and we sat there under a plastic sheet whilst the rain ate into the scenery. When I asked her if she'd seen Rex she told me that he was over at the Tower, near where she used to live. I must have looked surprised, because she said: 'Clogs don't come from nowhere, you know.'

And for the first time I really looked at her. 'Tell me about yourself,' I said, the words sounding foreign and unfamiliar because it wasn't something I'd ever said before.

'My name is Florence,' she said 'like the city in Italy where all the paintings used to be. I was an only child and my father died when I was quite young, but my mother managed to send me to a decent school. She couldn't afford health insurance for herself as well as schooling for me, so when she got ill that was that really. State care for six months, then on to the streets. What about you?'

'Me?' I hadn't expected her to ask about me.

'You must have gone to college. Was it wonderful?'

I remembered how blasé we'd all been about it, as though our privileged backgrounds had been something we'd created ourselves, brought into existence by our own outstanding merit. 'No,' I said slowly, thinking about it, 'it wasn't wonderful because we didn't appreciate any of it. We spent a great deal of time getting absolutely bombed and doing as little work as possible.'

'I didn't expect you to be so honest.'

'Neither did I.'

We both laughed and got to our feet. It was a short walk to the Tower, but a dangerous one. The path ran alongside an old canal, and an evil-smelling mist was rising with the dusk. We walked briskly, not looking too much to the left or right, but listening, listening all the time. We crossed the bridge without incident, skirted the multi-storey car park and entered the Tower by the subway.

I'd never been there of course. I'd heard about it, everyone's heard of the Tower, but it wasn't quite what I'd expected. The walls were covered with the most amazing graffiti – words, images, colours, designs, and the huge expanses of floor were filled with little polystyrene structures, all different, all individual, each one four square metres of home. They reminded me of snowflakes – superficially similar, profoundly different, and very, very white.

'They're not *all* white,' said Florence, 'take a look at that one.'

The owner had torn up little squares of old magazines, stuck them on to the outside of his computer crate and recreated a sun-lit park. The trunks of the plane trees were dappled with the distinctive yellow of those diptheria leaflets, and the deep-purple shadows were the unmistakable violet of budget condom packets. It was surprisingly effective, and I stopped to look.

'There's a really tremendous one round the corner,' Florence told me, so we went to see. The householder had managed to present the illusion of a window on the side of his box, with a vase of flowers on the sill and Victorian lace curtains, painstakingly cut from discarded tissue paper. The perspective of the room's interior was very clever, and I found myself smiling at a piece of representational art for the first time in years. I couldn't help it, I actually *liked* the thing, and I wondered what the interior of the box might have to offer. Box Art. It had a certain ring to it.

We found Rex without any difficulty. 'I believe you know someone called Enzo Andretti,' I began, realising that I hadn't planned this out as well as I might have done.

'Knew,' said Rex. 'Enzo's dead.'

For some reason I hadn't expected that. 'Listen,' I lied, 'I represent Cranford Smith, and I know you were trying to contact us. We're very interested in this unknown series of paintings by Donald Barnes, but we'd have to see them before we negotiated a price.'

'And who are you?'

'An employee.'

'I've already had a substantial offer, as it happens. Unseen.'

'From whom?'

The corner of Rex's mouth lifted in a smile. His eyes didn't change though. 'Twenty thousand new ecus. From Cranford Smith.'

'Ah.'

Florence looked at me accusingly, suddenly realising that I hadn't just not told her *all* the story, I hadn't really told her any of it.

'I was pursuing an independent line of inquiry,' I said, which rang about as true as the Environment Ministry's promises.

'Really.'

I couldn't hold his gaze, so I dropped my eyes. That was when I noticed his quilted boots, black with a dragon or a serpent or something embossed on the heels. I froze for a moment, which was the wrong thing to do, realised it, switched my gaze back to his face and found myself staring at his hair. It was dark, and close-cropped. Perfect, if you were thinking of wearing a wig.

I had to think quickly. Give up, go home and carry on working for Cranford for the next twenty years. Or bluff out a higher offer, and try to find a buyer for the series before I bought it myself. I could fiddle around with deposits – charge the buyer twice Rex's price, fifty per cent up front and the remaining fifty on receipt of the paintings.

Maybe Rex hadn't killed Enzo, and the boots were just a coincidence. Maybe he would be a nice, reliable person to do a deal with. Maybe.

'Twenty-five,' I said.

'Thirty.'

'Done.'

'There's an old boathouse by the side of the canal.'

'I know it.'

'Meet me there tomorrow, with the cash. Nine o'clock.'

'I'll need to hire a transporter. Donald's paintings could never be described as small.'

Rex laughed. 'Suit yourself.'

'How many pieces are there?'

'Forty-three.'

I swallowed. This was far better than I'd imagined. Less than a thousand each.

'Take it or leave it,' said Rex.

I said I'd take it.

I noticed Florence staring hard at Rex's boots, so I grabbed her by the hand and said, 'Let's go. I'll explain on the way out,' and I shepherded her towards the exit.

'He never used to have those boots,' said Florence.

I changed the subject.

'There's something not quite right about all this,' said Jennifer later.

'I've got a buyer,' I told her. 'Colonel Fitzpatrick, first one on the list of private clients I've been building up. It's amazing how greed can dispense with caution.'

'Isn't it,' said Jennifer.

'Do you think Rex killed Enzo?'

'Oh yes,' said Jennifer, 'Enzo was probably going to double-cross him, and do the deal with Cranford on his own. He must have known where the paintings were. And if he didn't mind killing Enzo he won't mind killing you either. Not once he's got the money.'

I hadn't thought about that.

'What shall I do?'

'Tell him you've left details of everything with me, and that if you're not back by a certain time I'll inform the militia. They'll be much more interested once they know the amount of money involved.'

That sounded reasonable.

'And one more thing,' said Jennifer, just as I was about to log out. 'Good luck. I think you're going to need it.'

★

The following night was a filthy night indeed. The wind was howling up and down the tower blocks like a demented were-wolf, and whipping the litter into violent eddies that would take the skin off your face if you got in the way. I manoeuvred the transporter through the traffic and out on to the canal road. There were no street lights along here, and the head-lamps cut a swathe through a dereliction that didn't comfort me in the slightest – Jennifer and her insurance policy seemed a long way away now. The boathouse loomed suddenly, big and black and decrepit, and I parked the vehicle as quietly as I could, which wasn't very quietly at all. The handbrake screamed like a banshee as I activated it, and when I cut the engine the whole thing shuddered a couple of times and made a noise that sounded like a death rattle. I picked up the canis-ter of money and climbed out of the cab.

I hung around outside for a few minutes, but nobody came. When it was ten past nine I took a deep breath, opened the lit-tle side door and went in. The interior of the boathouse was very quiet compared to the tumult of the elements outside. I flicked on my torch and moved the beam round in an arc. No paintings, just a couple of rotting canoes and a pile of ropes. A few packing cases. And a woman.

I was so surprised my mouth must have dropped open, because I remember inhaling some dust and coughing violent-ly. When I recovered she was standing in front of me, but she didn't look very friendly. I deduced this by the fact that she was pointing a gun at me, which turns out to be about the only thing I ever did deduce properly.

'You killa my husband,' she said.

'Killed,' I corrected automatically. Then, 'No, no, I didn't honestly, I'm not who you think I am.'

'You are Rex.'

'I'm not . . . you must be Mrs Andretti.'

'Señora Andretti.'

Why were we such sticklers for our respective languages?

'You think he double-cross you.'

'No, honestly.'

'You letta me hava my cut and I letta you go.'

'Señora Andretti, I came here to meet Rex myself.'

'Then where is he?'

I looked round the boathouse and shrugged. I was aware of her following my gaze and perhaps I could have jumped her then, but I didn't have the guts. The moment of silence that came after was broken by the scuffle of a shoe. We both turned towards the sound, peering into the darkness until I remembered the torch. The beam travelled slowly across the packing cases. Nothing.

'If that's you, Rex,' I said, 'we're ready to do a deal.'

There was a faint metallic scrape somewhere in front of us. If I'd had hackles they would have risen.

'Listen, Rex,' I said, trying to keep the panic out of my voice, 'there's someone called Jennifer who knows exactly where I am and what's been going on, and if I'm not back by a certain time she'll inform the militia, and considering the sum of money involved . . .'

'That really wasn't necessary,' said a voice behind me, 'I never intended to run out on you. However, I must insist on payment first, in full. Then I'll wait while you count the paintings. Is that satisfactory?'

I looked at Mrs Andretti. 'This,' I said, 'is Rex.'

She surveyed him for a moment. Then she said: 'You killa my husband.'

'He double-crossed me.'

She smiled, but without humour. 'He always was a bastard, my Enzo.' Then she turned to me. 'Fifty–fifty?'

It was still a good whack.

'Okay.'

There was the faint rasp of a match from beyond the packing cases, and then it flared. 'It's not okay at all,' said Cranford, standing up, a cigarette in one hand and a money canister in the other. 'I'll up the offer.'

'What is this, Piccadilly Circus?' I shouted, out of sheer frustration. 'What are you doing here?'

'The same as you, I imagine,' said Cranford.

'He come to see me yesterday,' said Mrs Andretti, 'in case I know where the paintings are. I read his computer while he go to the toilet. I think your Jennifer, she is a bit of a – how do you say – gossip. Nine o'clock at the old boathouse.'

'Forty thousand,' said Cranford to Rex.

Rex looked politely at me.

'He hasn't got anything like that sort of money,' said Cranford, 'he's bluffing.'

'Fifty,' said Mrs Andretti.

I glared at her.

'I've got a suggestion,' said Rex. 'Why don't you share them? Thirty thousand each, say. There's enough to go round, surely.'

We all looked at each other. 'All right,' said Cranford.

'Where are they?' said Mrs Andretti.

Rex smiled. 'Money first. I agree to sell to you, for the sum of thirty thousand new ecus each, a previously unknown series of paintings by the artist Donald Barnes, numbering forty-three separate pieces.'

Cranford and I handed over our canisters.

Mrs Andretti handed over her ammunition, but not her gun.

Rex handed over a small portfolio.

'What's this?' said Cranford, looking at it suspiciously.

'Forty-three paintings,' said Rex. 'Count them.'

Cranford placed the portfolio on the ground, and undid the clips. He hesitated a moment before he lifted the flap, then he pursed his lips and opened the portfolio right out.

It was full of watercolours.

The first one was of Hammersmith Bridge, swathed in mist, executed in diluted washes of Burnt Sienna and Payne's Grey. The next one was of Hyde Park in the dry season, with acres of dandelions and flowering bramble. The third one was an equally traditional view of Trafalgar Square, complete with rats. Cranford flipped through them, and in the bottom right-hand corner of each was the unmistakable signature of Donald Barnes.

Cranford looked up, grim-faced.

'They're genuine,' said Rex, 'I've got a magnifying glass if you want to examine the signature.'

'I know they're genuine,' said Cranford through clenched teeth. 'They're also worthless.'

140

'Oh I don't know,' said Rex, 'I think they're rather beautiful.'

'I can't sell these!' shouted Cranford. 'They negate everything the man stood for!'

'That,' said Rex over his shoulder as he walked away, 'is your problem.'

Mrs Andretti knelt down beside Cranford and picked up one of the paintings. 'He's right,' she said, 'they're beautiful. Sucha sensitivity. Sucha feeling fora the line. This was what he really wanted to paint.'

I joined them on the floor, spreading the thick sheets of paper around me in a fan. You could see the development, from some Turner-like abstracts back towards the representational.

'If these ever got out,' said Cranford, 'I'd be ruined. The Toenail Series is worth a fortune, and I've got more, a whole set of canvasses based on molars . . . To hell with the thirty thousand, these would cost me a lot more than that in the end. No,' he said, reaching into his pocket, 'this progeny cannot be allowed to survive.'

It was only when I saw the cigarette lighter in his hand that I realised what he was going to do.

'No!' I shouted. 'You can't do that! Half of them are mine anyway!'

'A quarter,' snapped Mrs Andretti, fiddling with something.

I pushed the portfolio across the floor with my foot. Cranford crawled after it, trying to get his lighter to work at the same time.

'You stoppa right there, Cranford,' said Mrs Andretti, levelling her gun at him.

'You've got no ammunition.'

'You think I giva Rex the whole bloody lot? You crazy?'

'Okay, okay,' said Cranford nervously, 'take them. Well, half of them. No, all of them. They're no use to me. But on one condition.'

'You maka me conditions?' Mrs Andretti waved her gun incredulously at Cranford, who cowered.

'I think I still need a job, señora,' I said, calculating how long it would take to repay the thirty thousand I'd borrowed from Colonel Fitzpatrick.

'Give me six months,' said Cranford, 'six months to sell everything I've got stored.' He looked at me. 'If I go bust so do you. Give me six months and then you can do what the hell you like with them, turn them into calenders or stick them on chocolate boxes, I don't care.'

'Give me the thirty grand then,' I said, 'I've got to repay Colonel Fitzpatrick.'

'You got Fitzpatrick to give you that up front?'

'He might prefer the watercolours.'

'All right,' snarled Cranford, 'but you have to give me six months.'

'It's a deal.'

In fact it only took Cranford four months to get the major retrospective organised, thanks to Jennifer. Mrs Andretti and I were invited to the preview. I took Florence with me as well. I'd been seeing quite a bit of her as I had plans to turn her into a receptionist when I opened my watercolour gallery, a sort of live-in assistant, if you see what I mean. Cranford said I was getting soft, offering a clog a roof over her head.

My gallery is going to be the most avant of the avant-garde. You see, I've decided to invent a whole new style of painting, the Post Organic School, where the artist uses that most basic medium of all, water. Once you've got it worked out semantically, you've cracked it.

Jennifer's been trying to persuade me to follow it up with an exhibition of Box Art. I asked her whether polystyrene crates counted as front rooms and kitchen walls, and she told me I was catching her drift and turning into a cool dude.

I have to admit that Cranford arranges these things with consummate skill. The paintings were hung in sequence round the gallery walls, and there was a nice little speech from Cranford about Donald Barnes's integrity, and his refusal to compromise his vision. There was also some very acceptable Indian wine, and an impressive array of seaweed dips.

Everyone was there, including the panel of experts from *Spot The Forgery*, and everyone was mightily impressed, except for Florence, Mrs Andretti and me. You see, not only did Cranford have the Toenail Series and the Molar Pieces up for sale, he had two hitherto completely unsuspected series of canvasses.

They were called *Pubic Hair with Dusting Powder* and *Eyelash with Mascara.*

The panel of experts thought they were great.

The Bad Mouse

Jane Shilling

I HAVE NEVER been able to understand those women who can't go shopping without a second opinion. The ones for whom the purchase of a hat, a handbag, a frock, is a democratic decision, a public event, a trial-by-jury in which the majority view is deemed to be correct. And yet it happens all the time. You hear them in the office on a Monday morning, talking about their Saturday: 'And then Sarah and I went to Harvey Nicks, and I nearly bought this amazing A-line shift in a sort of saffron shantung, but Sarah said, "Look, honestly, where would you *wear* it?" And I thought, well, she's got a point. There's no sense in buying it just because it's reduced from £399 to £200 in the sale if you're not going to get the use from it, so in the end I didn't, and we just went and had a glass of champagne instead . . .'

Well, frankly, you've only got to look at them to see where it gets them, this sort of sartorial group sex. Dressed by committee – and it shows. Though I did try it, once, quite recently, the communal shopping process. Just in case the clue to what I've been searching for might, against all expectations, be hidden somewhere there. I sacrificed an entire day; a great slice of my freedom (that is become so rare and precious that I dole it out to myself like some parsimonious eighteenth-century housewife dispensing a sprinkling of tea leaves from a locked caddy) deliberately given over to a shopping expedition with Janet from Copy-editing.

The event was planned with some precision. We were to meet in Soho, in a cavernous red-plush Chinese restaurant, where we would eat little doll's-house dishes of semi-nourishment designed to leave us sustained, but still hungry – prawns in crackly gold-and-ivory rice-paper vests; the braised feet of ducks with little balls of pinky-purple forcemeat bound to their ankles with pimpled thongs of skin; frilly fried fronds of dark-green seaweed; sharks'-fin dumplings like sagging suede purses filled with coral – before advancing on the West End in a sweeping movement that would start with Ally Capellino, move on to Marks & Spencer, Miss Selfridge and Wallis, then turn from the brawling grime of Oxford Street to the sweet, synthetic pastoral of Laura Ashley and Liberty before heading towards Bond Street and the exhilaration of pressing our hot noses against the cold, glittery, impregnable windows of Hermès and Gucci and Chanel.

As a plan, I didn't see how it could be improved. Over lunch, I even began to convince myself that I was on the brink of something; that doing in public what I had hitherto regarded as wholly private – sacramental, I suppose you could say – would somehow tear back the curtain; hand me the combination; lead me, in short, to the revelation that I had once spent so many weary Saturdays pursuing through the racks of expensive, cheap and sometimes downright sordid *schmutter* (oh, the gap-toothed zips, the prolapsed hemlines, the hanging shreds of sequins, the orange smears of foundation streaking across pearly *peau-de-soie* at the fag-end of the Harvey Nichols sale. You don't find anything as bad as that even in the Oxfam shop at World's End).

We rose from our table, congratulating ourselves on the meagreness of the bill, and crossed the street to Capellino, on whose sparse rails there hung chestnut and cloudy-grey organza wraps; skirts of crushed silk velvet flecked with spatters of gold; trailing robes of creamy crumpled linen, banded with stripes of pale-gold lamé mesh; rippling silvery surcoats fastened with knotted cords like the girdles of mendicant friars; tiny pelmet skirts of shaggy violet mohair, or creaking transparent PVC – all iridescent, like bubbles – and, in one corner, a skimpy wisp of sky-blue linen hung on a halter strap, scattered like a medieval meadow with white embroidered daisies.

'It's me,' I said to Janet. 'I'm going to try it on.'

I expect you know the dressing-rooms at Capellino. All very Designer Peasant – four wooden doors with iron sneck-latches, opening off a tiny stone-flagged corridor. And inside these little whitewashed cubicles, which I must say put me in mind of nothing so much as the outside loos at my old primary school – though without the branches of lilac growing in through the gap at the top of the door – they have stumpy wooden schoolroom chairs and iron hooks to hang your bag on – but not a mirror between them. You have to come out into the shop and look at yourself under the eyes of everybody. Asking for an opinion, really. It should have put me on my guard, if I'd thought about it, but once I saw the sky-blue and the daisies and the bias-cut simplicity of that dress, I didn't think. I just picked it up in size eight and hurried it off to the changing-room.

I shed my boots and my jodhpurs and my layers of jumpers and cardigans and vests and T-shirts (it was February, and bitter outside, though the Spring collections were just in). I slung the halter strap around my neck and wrapped the ties around my waist and strutted, swinging my hips a bit, just to feel the flirt of the little flared skirt, and I stood in front of the mirror, thinking about how that blue would look when there'd been some sun to turn my skin and hair gold, with a pair of sandals with a tiny heel, nothing extreme: just a narrow bobbin with barely-there straps in silver-gilt, perhaps, or milk-white, with toenails and lips painted a sort of pinky-beige, and I suppose I must have been in this little reverie for about five seconds when Janet said:

'Oh, what a shame, it doesn't fit, does it?'

'What?' I said. I was shocked. I think I'd forgotten she was there. 'What do you mean?'

'Here,' she said, taking a handful of the material. 'Across the back. It's far too big. You just don't fill it. You and it are different shapes. It was made for someone else. If you don't believe me,' she added, looking rather frightened (I'd twitched myself out of her grasp – I don't much care for being handled, on the whole – and I may have given her a look. I do that sometimes, without really meaning to), 'then turn round and see for yourself.'

I looked at my reflection in the mirror then, and I saw myself as I was, standing there in my wrinkled socks, in the steely February light in that cold, bare shop, with my face pinched and grey-mauve from the cold and my nose all shiny from lunch and my legs and arms sticking out from that azure dress, goose-pimpled and fuzzed with sticky-out hairs like gooseberries, and the back of the frock (she was absolutely right) gaping across my own, much narrower back – to say nothing of the front, from whose wrapover *décolletage* my upper ribs and collarbones rose like the yellowing keys of an old harpsichord. I went back to the dressing-room, put the frock back on its hanger, resumed my wintry layers of black knitting, told Janet the sharks'-fin must have disagreed with me and caught the bus straight home to World's End.

Mum was there, looking after little Sergei (Why is he called that? they always ask. Nobody's business but mine, I always say). Of course, she wanted to know what had become of my longed-for shopping expedition, but I wasn't about to explain myself to her. I wasn't even sure I could explain it to myself. So I muttered something about not finding anything I fancied at the price and showed her out the door, though she was half-way through feeding Sergei his Petits Filous. Then I stuffed Sergei into his Bonpoint pyjamas – the creamy brushed-cotton *toile de Jouy* ones with ivory ric-rac around the neck and the wrists and ankles, and the little pink and green shepherds and shepherdesses with tumbling curls and knots of ribbons on their crooks tending their sheep all over them – and hustled him off to bed. He didn't say anything. He never does. Doesn't even cry much these days, now he's not really a baby any more. It's one of the things I like best about him. That and how beautiful he is. All curly and rosy and silent and peaceful, just like one of the shepherd boys on his pyjamas.

I sat in the rocking-chair next to his bed, rocking backwards and forwards, backwards and forwards, reading the *Two Bad Mice* – I love those mice, the violence of them, smashing and stealing all those lovely things belonging to those dolls too stupid to understand the value of what they've got – and after Sergei went to sleep I sat on in the dark, thinking about what had gone wrong.

The waste of the day was vexing, of course. But not in itself significant. A risky experiment, conducted rather against my better judgement, had turned out badly. For Janet's opinion I gave, naturally, not a fig. What disturbed me was that tiny gap in time through which, for a moment, she and I had both seen my bare, forked person protrude in such ugly fashion. It made me wonder.

Wondering, until Sergei came along, had not been much on my agenda. Scarcely a moment of my time, before him, that was not devoted to thinking about clothes. The wardrobes are full of them now – all those other mes, suspended docilely from their hangers, waiting to be allowed out. The *crêpe-de-Chine* Conran shirt with the huge, flying collar, hidden like a sleeping archangel among a nasty clutch of business woman's hard-edged white polycotton in the Simpson's sale; the starched New Look Swiss voile shirtwaist with its yards of crackling starched skirts, scattered with penny-sized white embroidered dots – a crumpled heap of Nattier-blue rags when I came upon it bundled at the back of a crammed rail in Cornucopia; the pale-pink kid swagger coat lined in pigeon's-breast grey-pink satin; the Persian lamb three-quarter-length jacket with the black velvet pockets and stand-up collar of silvery mink found lurking amid mephitic tweeds in the incontinent old-woman reek of the Oxfam shop – all snatched, like hostages, or sprung like prisoners from under the noses of their ignorant guards, the shop-girls. But what's to become of them now, all my as-yet-undiscovered other selves? And what's to become of me?

When I knew that Sergei was coming, I understood that things would be different; that adjustments would have to be made. But it seemed like a problem that could be dealt with as I am accustomed to meet most setbacks – by force of will and self-discipline. I was surprised, and not very pleased, to find him on the way, but once I'd got used to the idea that there was someone else living in there, I thought I'd carry on much as before. I knew I wasn't going to be one of those women who see pregnancy as the ideal opportunity to succumb to a lifetime's tendency to look like a floral-print binbag full of partly-set cement. I spent the whole nine months wrapped in the tight black Lycra embrace of a Conran stretch bodysuit, whose only points of entry were at the neck, wrists and ankles. You had to take the whole thing off every time you wanted to pee, but it was worth it. Sending a message, you might say. Though you might also say that it was a bit late for that particular message.

The day he was born, I had a premonition. I set off on a kind of valedictory circuit of my old haunts – as though I knew I'd not be back and needed to find something before I left. And I knew what it was, when I saw it, ranged demurely next to the neat little pastel separates in the Anne Klein concession at Harvey Nichols. A black leather jacket – all over zips, with great gold nuggets for buttons. Tough, it was. And carefree. The sort of thing you could wear to roar out of your own life and on to the next thing, on the back of some man's motorbike. Not me at all, in fact. Except that it was so soft. Softer than new skin. And it smelt of vanilla and of the baby lotion that stood, with its irritating air of expectation, on what had once been my dressing-table, but was now a shrine-in-waiting to the obstinate tenant of my insides.

When I put it on, of course, the brass-zipped edges wouldn't meet across my front. I was standing there in the muslin-draped dressing-room, watching in the full-length mirror the sea-monster ripplings of my black Lycra abdomen as the baby grappled tetchily back and forth, trying to find a comfortable position (or, as it later turned out, the exit), when the *vendeuse* came in and gave me a look. Not the look I was getting used to saleswomen giving me – the one of panicky surmise that they might at any moment be called upon to do something absolutely revolting involving hot water and piles of pristine Calvin Klein T-shirts – but a steady, assessing sort of look. She examined my reflection in the glass and for a moment I had the feeling that she could see what I saw: a little figure, speeding away in that Marie-Antoinette version of a biker's jacket, faster and faster down a long, straight track towards a vast, glittering, deep-blue horizon. Then she said, 'You'd better take it. It'll remind you, when you're pushing the pram.'

So I did. I wrote the cheque, and I carried the bag home

and hung the jacket on the door, and then I sat down on the bed and said, 'OK, you can come out now.'

Since then, I find I don't care to go hunting any more. It isn't precisely that there is no time. On the contrary, the child-haunted hours of evening and weekend hang festooned around me like Spanish moss. On Saturday and Sunday I push the baby to the park and sit watching in the harsh city sunshine while he pulls up the daisies or throws crumbs to the quarrelling starlings; each weekday after work I sit here in the dimming twilight by his cot, waiting for I've no idea what. Nothing stops me from planning, searching, plundering the pages of *Vogue* for other selves – just as I always did. Except that time seems not to belong to me any more.

Sometimes I turn a page, or glimpse a shop window from the top of the bus, and for a moment, I think I catch sight of something; there is that familiar tight, fluttery feeling – of the future, waiting for me, just within my grasp. But something is missing. The speed, the stealth, the ferocity of desire have gone. Where once a square inch of material would urge *Take me, I am your destiny*, now the echo comes back *You know who you are. We can't help you any more.*

I look at Sergei, lying in his cot like a Bronzino princeling, breathing quietly in the light from the street lamp, dreaming like one of the little shepherd boys roaming Arcady on his pyjamas. Well, who am I, then? I think. The death's head in the daisy-scattered halter-neck? Or the little figure fleeing down the straight track towards the unknown? In that moment, an idea comes to me. But for the time being, I just carry on rocking, and thinking, and rocking, and thinking . . .

Nine Lives

Shaun Levin

WE CLEAR THE dishes away in silence.

I say: 'I'll have dessert later.' Because I don't think I can stand one more second at the table with you.

Then we move over to the living-room, where the light is brighter. It's easier to read in here. Easier to read than in the bedroom, say. So I stretch out on the sofa and get back to my book. That ceiling fan you installed last summer whirrs around lazily. The constant background hum makes it easier to focus on the page.

And then. And then you say: 'What?' From your armchair across the carpet. You say that, and expect me to come up with an answer. You play with the cat you brought home three weeks ago. That white, hairy, deaf Persian cat with the tail like a.

'What did you say?'

'Is everything okay?'

'Oh, yes,' I say. 'I'm just trying to finish this story.'

So I carry on reading. I've been ploughing through this book for God knows how long. Still ten more stories to go. Though it seems like I'll never get through them all. That's the problem when you can't keep your mind on one thing. There's never an end in sight.

You're still staring at me from the other end of the carpet as the cat settles down on your lap. And you start doing that thing with your leg, jiggling it up and down. I know exactly what you're trying to tell me. Let's go, let's go. Let's get a move on, you'll say. I'll look over at you and say: You know, that's really irritating, that thing you're doing with your leg. Please stop it. And then you'll make one of those faces of yours, and I'll say, it's not as if I'm asking for much. Am I?

The cat's fast asleep by now, its bum against your stomach, that tail hanging like a pendulum. Its head on your knee. The lazy shit. It isn't even bothered by your knee bouncing up and down like that.

'Is everything okay?' you ask.

'Oh, yes, fine,' I say. 'I told you, everything's fine.'

'Fine?'

'Yep, fine.'

What a stupid game. If only I could concentrate I'd get to the end of this one in no time. But not with you here in the room. I wish I could just say: You know, why don't you just get out. Just go. Just give me some room in here.

'Let's do something,' you say.

'Like what?'

'I don't know,' you say. 'Anything.'

'I just want to finish this story,' I tell you. 'I'd rather just stay in here and finish the story.'

But I will change my mind if you insist. I will. Just tell me that we have to go to a movie. Now. That we have to go to a movie or for a walk. This minute. Or that you've made plans and there's no way we can cancel.

Oh, fuck it.

It's so bloody hot in here. I can already feel the sweat tickling the underside of the skin on my forehead. Maybe I can keep it in, somehow, mind over matter. But you can't fool sweat, you know. You can't tell the body what to do. The body has a life of its own. And there goes the cat. Sliding down on to the floor. It gives me one of its looks and then slouches back on to your lap.

'Did you see that?' you say.

'See what?'

'The cat.'

'What about the cat?' I say.

'I think I'm going to go for a walk,' you say.

So you get up and walk to the door. Fine. That's fine. The cat looks at you, sulkingly. It's not at all pleased to have had its cushion taken away.

'I'm taking a key,' you say.

So just take it and go.

The door shuts behind you like a punch in the tummy and then there's silence. Reading is easier now. This is better. Yes. Listen. Peace and quiet at last. Things can be so still when you're alone. If only it wasn't so stifling in here. And sticky. Time to invest in an air-conditioner. That's the next item on the list. But first you'd better find a new job. A proper nine-to-five job this time. One that'll pay for more than just our day-to-day existence. The sweat comes off my forehead in the palm of my hand and I massage my neck and bring my hand down to my chest. The hairs are brittle with dampness. Everything's so moist and humid. There'll be an oval sweat-stain on the sofa when I get up. Fuck. Summers never used to be like this.

Good idea. Iced coffee. Treat yourself for once. Relax more. Take some time to gather your thoughts. Come on cat, let's have some iced coffee. Let's take a walk from the living-room to the kitchen. What a lovely walk. Stretch our bones. If I went out looking, I'd know where to find you. I know where I'd go on a night like this. The last time I followed you there we were like strangers. Watching you let that boy cruise you among the trees made me feel left out. As if I was to blame somehow for what was happening to us. As if I could have put a stop to it all and got things back on the right track. As if I could have taken your hand and led you back home.

I fill the kettle and wait for the faint hiss. I pour some of the water back into the sink. There's no air in this kitchen. The tiny window's no help. The smell sticks to the walls and snakes its way into the cupboards. I must get a lid for this rubbish bin. It's a cesspool in here. The garlicky smell from the dishes in the sink. And there won't be any clean teaspoons. I just know it. The milk in the fridge'll be sour. And it's been two weeks, you know, two weeks, probably even more, since we last went to the supermarket. We should paint the kitchen walls again. The grease around the cooker needs to be wiped and the spot where the rain came in last winter has gone all mouldy. Hot sweat and soap fumes rise up from my chest. Oh fuck, not another summer of this. Please, not another whole fucking summer.

Just abandon yourself. That's what you said. I'd brought you home for the first time and we were standing here, in the kitchen, and you said: Just abandon yourself to the heat. Just give in.

You wore that white vest, damp with sweat-marks under your armpits. How could it have been so. Your dark nipples showing through the thin fabric. I watched you earlier that night in the bar. Laughing at everyone's jokes. How they all wanted to impress you and fill your silences with their offerings. You stayed behind after your friends had left and waited for me to come over. You thought I'd want to impress you, too, didn't you? But you were the one who was impressed. You were. You told me so. You did. What a handsome man, you said. Your eyes are so. So.

I made iced coffee for us when we got home. You said: Not too much milk for me thanks. It makes my throat go all phlegmy. Then you came and hugged me from behind. The humidity made my back stick to you. We must have been naked by then. So quick we were. Diving into intimacy like undernourished. Like undernourished children. And I wanted to say: That feels so good. Let me put my head into the hollow of your neck. Right there. Let me lick the beads of sweat off your upper lip. And I watched all evening to see if you'd wipe them away. But you never did. You didn't seem to notice them.

The water clicks off.

I just can't be bothered any more.

And then we went to the Heath. Remember. You said: A council flat right by the Heath. You lucky bastard. And we laughed, like conspirators. Just look how those first few days keep coming back to me like a possibility. You were kind that morning when you stayed for breakfast, I remember, and gentle. Pass the butter please. And the jam, please. Come on, stop looking at me like that. Please don't. I'm the one who should be staring, you said.

We spent the day together. I lent you an old pair of swimming trunks. You said: Maybe I should go home and get my own. But I said: These look fine on you. It's a pity to miss the sun. Now's the best time to catch a tan.

We spread our towels out on the grass by the water. I lay on my back and closed my eyes and imagined us alone. No one there to bother us. And then I must have laughed, I know I did, because you asked me what was so funny, and I might have said I was just being paranoid. Or perhaps I touched your shoulder and you said: Oh, that smile of yours. It's. It's.

There goes your cat. Crawling off the armchair and gliding towards the living-room door. It turns to look at me and then waits for you to come in. The cat stares at the front door. It can sense your keys, but I can hear them wrestling with the lock. Then you open the door and I see how dark it is behind you.

'Nice outside?'

'Oh, great,' you say. 'I went for a swim.'

'A swim,' I say. 'Out there in the dark?'

'It was nice,' you say. 'I was the only one there.'

You're framed in the doorway now, your hands in your pockets. Oh, you beautiful man. You beautiful, beautiful man. Too beautiful for me. And the cat comes to sit beside me and keeps its eyes on you. Come and pick it up. Can't you see it wants to rest on your lap.

'I brought you some chocolate,' you say.

'I'll have it in the morning.'

'Are you coming to bed?'

Oh please don't.

'Soon,' I say. 'I'll be there soon.'

Please.

You stand there deliberating whether to come in or not. Should I. Should I not. And the bright yellow petals. I see the bright daisy petals tossed about the room. I push the cat off the sofa and go back to my book. You know I'm in the middle of this story.

'Still on the same one?' you say.

I try not to hear you walk away, shower, piss, turn off the light in the bathroom, in the bedroom, by the bedside. And sleep.

Wait. Just wait a bit. Slow down. Let him sleep. And then it's

161

quiet again. It is. It is. It is. But everything is contaminated by now. The noise spreads everywhere and into everything. There's no point in trying to finish the story if I can't concentrate. Best just go to bed. Take a shower and get into bed.

I let the hot water massage the back of my neck, soften my muscles. I can forget the heat out there for a while. I used to like sitting here on the shower floor, watching you on the toilet, trying to get you all excited. I can't imagine touching your body now. Just the thought of your sour smell makes me want to be sick. I wash the soap off and stand in front of the mirror, trying to see myself through the mist. I rub the towel over my skin. Pointless, really, as I'll only be sweating again in no time. I hang the towel up and go to bed.

The covers are on the floor and you're lying on your back. Your cock semi-hard with sleep. I touch your side, accidentally, with my elbow, and whisper: 'I'm sorry.' You mumble something, only pretending to have been woken. I lie on my stomach, facing you. You know not to open your eyes. You wouldn't dare. You let me look at you as much as I want to. As much as I need to. How can you feel so safe in here? How can you just lie there and know that no harm will come to you?

'Where to?' you ask.

'Oh,' I say. 'It's just too fucking hot in here.'

'It's late.'

'I know. But I'm hungry.'

'Have some chocolate.'

Fine.

'I will.'

'Good night then.'

I leave the light off in the kitchen. I boil the water and feel around in the cupboard for the coffee and the sugar. I take a mug down from the shelf. There aren't any clean teaspoons. Not one fucking teaspoon. I'm not going to dig around in the sink. I use my fingers to put what feels like two coffees and two sugars into the mug. I lick the sugar off my fingers and a grain of coffee sticks to my tongue. The light in the fridge isn't working, and the bloody milk is off. Best get back to the story. Just so I can say: I did it. I started the story and I finished it and now I can go on. But your snoring follows me. You snore.

162

Softly. Drip after drip. Please. Please. For God's sake stop. Why can't everything just shut the fuck up.

'Russell,' you call.

What.

'Come to bed.'

Don't. Please don't.

I'll just sleep here on the couch like I used to. You know how I hated having someone else in my bed. But I was always too. Always too. To tell them to leave. They'd sleep in my bed and mess up my sheets and leave their aftershave on my mattress. And then I'd have to throw everything in the wash and start all over again. But now you're in the bed and the couch has been taken over as well. The cat keeps its eyes tightly shut and stretches out even more.

Just a few more lines, then the last line, and that's it. The story's over. Finished. On the way back to bed I remember the night Peter came to stay. It was one of the first of these hot summers and we couldn't fall asleep. We agreed that the only way to bring an end to the day was to fuck, so we did, and I thought: At least now the day doesn't have to go on for ever. So, now, when I get back to you, when I get back to bed, and there's no choice but to sleep, you look at me.

'What's the matter?' you say.

'What?'

'We can talk if you like.'

Oh, for fuck's sake.

'No, no. Just sleep.'

'Good night.'

Go. Please go. Please. Just go. Please. Please. Please. Just go. Just leave. Please. Please.

Don't touch me. Don't.

'Are you okay?'

Your hand touches the dampness on my stomach.

'Get some sleep,' you say. 'Try and get some sleep.'

It must be almost morning by now. The air's a little cooler, and it's so quiet out there. I stroke your back and curl up at your side. A memory comes to me: A mustard-coloured carpet and my mother on the floor beside my bed. She would read to me every night. Sometimes she'd finish the story before I'd fallen sleep, and then she'd ask me if she could go now. And I'd say: Yes. Yes, you can go now.

Rapunzel

Daphne Rock

RAPUNZEL BRUSHES HER hair on the corner of Armoury Way and the High Street. It is tangle-free and swings round her face like a spun plumb-line. Her face is often hidden inside its Anglo-Saxon gilt. Rapunzel clings to the beauty of her hair like a sky diver to the rip-cord. Prince says he would like to swing on her hair. Fuck that, says Rapunzel. Prince, encouraged, asks if all her hair is silky, straight and gold. Rapunzel's laugh almost hides her rage.

Prince has little hair on show, but what he has is neatly incised with sharp circles of scalp. If I swung on your hair, says Prince, I'd fly. They lounge over the pavement, messing up the bus queue. A woman loaded with Tesco bags tells them to get out of the bloody road. They move, lazily as they can, to sit on the wall. Old cow, says Rapunzel. They both gaze at the cars jammed by the red light, and then the 44 bus, loading slowly with grey people in beige macs and deformed feet. The woman with the Tesco bags slips slightly as she hoists herself on board.

Prince pushes her off the wall and she hits back at him. They scatter the pedestrians, some of them are scared. Rapunzel shakes her hairbrush and Prince starts running away, sprinting for the High Street, turning to taunt her as he stops on the brink of the kerb, scaring a fast car. The driver yells out of his window, move your butt, wog, as he accelerates away. Prince's face goes hard and he turns his back on Rapunzel as she moves close. Shut your stupid games, he says. See you tonight.

Rapunzel watches him slouch away, the brightness going out of her face. She crosses when the lights change and lets herself into the block. Lift working. Lights working. Some miracle. She can hear her flat before she gets to the door which is, as usual, propped half-open with Tilly's trike. She hears her mum screaming at Tilly and when she sees Rapunzel she starts screaming at her too, just because she's there, and Rapunzel's mum would rather shut Tilly in her room, come down and get at the gin. While she's still sober she thinks Rapunzel doesn't know, but she knows.

On the street with Prince, Rapunzel is sixteen years old and doesn't care; in the flat she's a beast of burden and keeps chipping her fingernails. There's another time, which floats just inside her skull, where Rapunzel is a princess and the kind man is there, the one she dreams about and believes in, now and then. He makes her wooden toys: not dolls but animals and wagons and trees, and they play with them together on the floor. He calls her by her name, draws her pictures of castles in forests and winged horses. He brushes her hair and tucks her into bed with her wooden toys and pulls a red blanket over her. He gives her a prickly kiss on her cheek, and she sleeps, every night, deeply.

Now she does not sleep well, and everyone calls her Zel and she rubbishes her dreams. Some fool must have fed her fairy stories as a baby she thinks, and left out the nasty bits.

Rapunzel kicks the trike aside and shuts the door. For God's sake, they don't have to live in the pocket of all the snobs living on the fifth floor. Everyone knows that her mum drinks and Tilly screams and Zel goes with niggers. No need to let them see it all in action. It's a small hall and Rapunzel kicks her way through the litter of dirty clothes and plastic bags and the sweet papers Tilly has cast aside. Her mum's been at it already. She's wearing the red mini-skirt and halter-top and the room is a tip. Chip bags and dirty cups, telly on full blast and Tilly's wet nappy on the table.

She should be out of nappies, Rapunzel says. You ought to give her a chance. She'll be one of those problem kids. Like you, says Rapunzel's mum. Rapunzel doesn't reply and starts clearing up. She switches the telly off and bundles the nappy into the kitchenette. Her mum puts the telly back on. You're just like a problem kid yourself, says Rapunzel. Her mum pours some more gin, she's already past caring what Rapunzel notices, and starts giving funny little coughs. Sometimes Rapunzel thinks her mum is mental. Maybe all mums are mental. Only her mum acts very strange; one day she stays in bed; the next she runs around in her silly little girl clothes and shrieks with laughter. Rapunzel hears her in the night, up and down, singing and coughing. Rapunzel is afraid for Tilly when her mum is like this. She wonders if her mum was ever young and hopeful and flirted on street corners, and what turned her into the slag she is, who is no use to anyone and wouldn't be missed, except perhaps by the gossips of the fifth floor. Maybe she's not so far gone tonight, she can talk.

You been out with that Prince?

What if I have, says Rapunzel.

I don't want you going with coloureds. Can't think what you see in them. You're the last one in the world to go with coloureds, Zel.

Rapunzel flares, don't call me Zel. I'm not Zel. My dad called me Rapunzel.

Her mum lurches and spills a little gin. She points a finger crowned with a yellow tin ring. Don't you call that pimp a dad.

Rapunzel moves out of range of the gin. He didn't drink himself silly.

Didn't have to. Her mum hears Tilly give a single, piercing wail, and sways across to kick the door shut. Got what he wanted stone cold sober.

You went with him, Rapunzel says. That's how you got me, isn't it.

Rapunzel's mum puts her head on one side and looks cunning. I was having a good life before I got you back. Snively brat you were, too. Went on and on about your Prince. Princes, Princes. All Princes.

Rapunzel picks up Tilly's T-shirt and her hands pleat it and fold it. She wants to be cool. Get answers. Wants to put this pathetic little drunk in its place and talking sense for once.

169

Seems that's what your dad told you to call him. Dirty bugger.

I'm sixteen, says Rapunzel. You ought to tell me. Why you had me, why you left him, why you got me back. Seems you people treated me like fucking lost luggage. Then gave me some pills to make me forget for a hundred years. People aren't meant to forget. Rachel, she was in care, she's got a big book of pictures. Where's my pictures. Where's me when I'm a kid. Where's your wedding photo. It's like I'm dead.

It isn't what she has meant to say. She has meant to be cool, adult. She feels a bit like Tilly must feel. Tilly is still sending out short fog siren wails, muffled slightly by the door. Upstairs will be banging soon.

But Rapunzel's mum has had too much gin. She slips and knocks a fairground dog off the mantelpiece. It smashes on the floor and she starts to cry. It's true though, Rapunzel thinks. I got born at thirteen.

She remembers an enormous teddy bear with a little straw hat and a real T-shirt and striped shorts. The man keeps it in a big room. A room where she has her breakfast because she remembers that the teddy has a plate and a bowl and breakfast beside her. One day . . . yes, one day she takes him in the bath when the man is getting her nightclothes ready, and he turns greyish, shrunken and ugly. The man tries to dry him and fluff him out, but he never fits his clothes again, and Rapunzel sits beside an empty chair. The man says he will get her a new one but he never does, and she is glad, because the old one is gone for ever and can't be replaced.

She has another go at her mum who has gone like that teddy bear, small and shrunken and ugly, slumped by the sofa. I'm sick of being told lies, she says. She goes across to shake her mum up, make her head sick, but she can't do it.

She picks up the thin body and rolls it on to the sofa. Then she goes to find Tilly who has stopped crying and who lies wide awake, her brown eyes dull and worn as old pennies. Rapunzel pulls the blanket over her arms, the skin brown and dusty with little dark slashes where she's fallen over and scarred, then says on an impulse, do you miss your dad, Tilly. Tilly stares, as if Rapunzel is talking foreign, then reaches under the blanket and pulls out her monkey puppet. Dad, she says, dad. Rapunzel feels her blood rise with anger against the skinny, drunk doll on the sofa. What's she going to do with them both. Or with herself. Sixteen years old, no job, stuck on the fifth floor of the Arndale with an alco and a mong. Oh pet, she says to Tilly who is going drowsy and happy with company, oh pet.

She brushes her hair and changes her earrings, sprays herself with the perfume she nicked from Arding's, and sits on the bed looking at herself in the mirror until Tilly drops off. She looks okay in the mirror. Just as well she's learned to shoplift, though a lifetime of nicking stuff from shops so that she can look good doesn't sound much fun. People always get caught in the end. Time'll come, she'll end up like her mum, give up. Rapunzel doesn't think she'll mind tinting her hair, blondes can keep it going for years and years anyway. It's the not being someone that gets her in the gut. She plays at being Prince's girl, white girl gets black guy, plays sexy and cool, but she knows she's only pretending, it isn't going to change anything. Years and years in the Arndale, fighting the cockroaches and the muck on the stairs and the smell of the chutes, like she's been labelled rubbish from the word go.

She goes out. She thinks about fairy stories, about princesses shut up in castles in forests guarded by evil witches and waiting for princes to come and rescue them. Bollocks, Rapunzel says to the evening air, looking up at the tower block, just recently painted all nice blue and white as if it really is pretending to be a fairy castle. Castles in the air. That's what the Council ad said. Buy your own castle in the air. Fancy anyone even thinking the poor little drunk doll could buy a decent washing machine, let alone a flat pretending to be a castle. Rapunzel twitches her shoulders so that the white blouse, the one she has done by hand because the launderette turns them grey, falls a little over her arms. Princesses always have white arms she thinks, but the girls she goes out with are beautiful black. Polished. She wonders why she goes for black and Prince for white.

She takes a bus up to the Junction. It is a bright evening, time to be young. She knows where to find the girls, the posse will be along later. They are all black except Rapunzel, but she is welcome. There won't be any white boys when they join up, but Prince is lord. If Prince chooses Zel, that's okay.

Everyone hears the posse approaching. It's as if the Junction has been lit up with fireworks and music. Soon the pavement overflows with them all, laughing and pushing and the tape pounding out songs. People cross the road, and not so much because there isn't room. The older black couples, just finished shopping, look vexed. The whites simply freeze up into their pasty skins. Rapunzel watches for Prince but it's late, he won't come now. The girls try to pull her along with them, but she is too proud to tag behind and swings her gold hair dismissively. Can't stop, she says, looking at her watch and giving LeRoy a sideways, flirty look, just to show Prince is not on her mind.

She starts walking, away from the bright sun. She walks through some flats and before long she reaches the gardens by the community hall where she sits down and seriously considers herself. She looks at her fingers and the palms of her hand. She's so white you'd think she'd been washed by hand too. That dad, she thinks. Wonders how her pastry-white mum got Tilly. Not that it matters, the whole world being the big blur that it is, but why can't her mum answer one question, just one. Maybe she is pissed most of the time but it's like she's being wicked, keeping Rapunzel in the dark, waiting for her to go mad too so that they're all three screaming mad and might as well jump under a bus. Just one question, was the man her dad or Tilly's dad because he sure as hell can't be both.

If Rapunzel keeps her eyes screwed shut against the bright sky she sees pictures. In this one she is wearing a long white dress, which is awkward on the stone stairs. On a table there are some ripe mangoes and a knife with a pearly handle. She is looking out of a window, which is so high that the tree tops are below her and she can see the road twisting away from her tower to disappear into the mountains. There are heavy steps coming nearer and before she can reach for the knife she turns to see a black hand dangling a gold chain, a belcher, the one she has always desired.

Rapunzel wakes in a blind panic, jumping to her feet, her

mouth open ready to scream. The footsteps belong to a work-
man spiking litter forty yards away. She forces her mouth shut
with one hand and sits back on the metal seat. A fire engine
screams down York Road. For a moment she thinks mum has
set the flat on fire, gets up to run, then tells herself to be sensi-
ble. She must be still dreaming because there is Prince, walking with his head down, very fast, as if he thinks all Babylon is
going to turn up any minute. He doesn't see her, passes on,
and she is not sorry because she can't at this moment imagine
being the girl he enjoys, all buzz and fizz and let the rest of the
world go fuck itself. I don't love Prince she thinks. If I did, I'd
care. Prince isn't going to make it to brain surgeon or high
court judge. He'll do time in Feltham like the rest of them.
Come out on a rehab programme and go steady in panel beating. Get a flat in the Arndale and be faithless to a load of
women.

The sun has gone down and she'd better move.

How could a person forget years of her life. There's a small
shutter in her brain that blinks briefly on old scenes, otherwise
she'd believe she doesn't really exist at all and that right now,
this minute, she is nothing but someone else's dream. And
how, if she is a real person, has she got by so long without
questioning that huge gap before Tilly was suddenly there in
the pram and they were in the Arndale flat. She's asked her
mum once and got some crazy stuff about how she's been
almost dying with pneumonia and that makes people forget all
sorts of things. Why has she trusted her mum who is obviously some sort of nut. You have to trust someone, don't you.
Only now she doesn't have anyone to trust. She can't go on
pretending to be smart and sexy and streetwise with Prince
when inside she is like a – she searches for a comparison –
mess of unravelled knitting.

Her steps sound loud as she hurries down towards the Town
Hall. She wears heavy black lace-ups which she has bought
with cash nicked from her mum's purse. More sense than
wasting it on gin and there's Tilly's red jumper she's bought
too because it isn't easy to steal from the children's-wear
department, what with the rich mothers all over the place
pawing through the merchandise with gold-ringed fingers.

She hasn't made love with Prince. Like all the rest of the posse, he's longing for a kid of his own but she's seen what happens, off to another woman once she's pregnant and then he's free, popping in to deliver an occasional toy when he's in funds and got time. Something else stops her, she can't explain it, just a feeling.

She's always a bit scared, going up to the flat at night, even though they've got entry phones. The doors don't shut very well, they're not foolproof. The lift is still working and it doesn't look like the flat's burned down. She tries to laugh at herself and it comes out tinny, sorrowful. Rapunzel has decided never to get moany, she's seen what it's done to her mum. She is cross with the sorrowful sort of laugh and goes in quickly, peeps at her mum, still flat out on the sofa, and then checks Tilly. There's dried tears on her cheeks and Rapunzel spits on a tissue and rubs at them.

In bed, her head half under the pillow, she feels a despair so deep it's like a knife in her belly. How's Tilly ever going to do at school? How are the teachers going to deal with her mum, who won't tell them how Tilly is because she doesn't know. If it comes to it she'll pretend she's Tilly's mum. Tilly's a human being. Deserves, whatever her mum and dad. Bloody fairy-tales Rapunzel thinks. Bloody parents.

She wakes up, suddenly, a long time later and listens. Cars, planes, a few odd shouts. Tilly's little snores. Thump of music from two floors up. Then it comes. 'Rapunzel. Rapunzel.' She dives under the bedclothes. God's sake, the devil has come for her. She wakes up a little more and listens again. 'Rapunzel.' She gets up and opens the window, the couple of inches permitted. The Town Hall doesn't want its tenants committing suicide out of its own windows. Make sure they go somewhere else. She screws up her eyes. There's someone down there. A big guy. 'Rapunzel' floats up again.

She's scared sick. First because she doesn't know who it is, second because people will start looking out soon and it's bad enough being their family without strange men calling her out at night.

She remembers. No one knows her name. She's made sure to keep it secret. Her dad gave her her name and no one is going to make fun of that. Couldn't be her dad down there, could it. Actually, Prince knows her name.

She talks to herself in her head. If it's your dad or Prince down there what's worrying you? She shivers. Could be where I stop being anyone. She risks waking Tilly and puts the light on, goes to the window and shakes her hair so that it spins back and forth under the light, signalling. Then she pulls on her jeans and shirt and slips out of the flat.

It is never truly dark around the Arndale. She is frightened here at night, the irregular cars and huge shadows and unnatural noises. She moves slowly away from the entry doors, and gives a small scream of dismay when a heavy arm lands on her shoulders. It's me, says a voice in her ear, and the arm propels her round the corner towards King George's Park, they walk like clockwork toys until Prince lifts her over the railings then vaults them himself. He drags her under the trees and makes her lie down. He gags her mouth with his hand as she tries to speak. Gotta keep your voice down. It's like a distorting mirror, being with Prince in the dark under trees and both of them shaking with fear. She struggles a bit but Prince keeps his hand firmly in place. What the hell is going on?

Trouble, says Prince. Seven of us down Tooting with Eddy. He started it. Out of his head on something. Got everyone worked up. Next thing there's a knife and he's on the ground. All blood and stuff. Looked like he was dead.

Rapunzel bites the hand over her mouth and it moves enough to release her voice. What did you do?

Scarpered, of course. Rapunzel forgets she is scared. You left him, she whispers. Phoned the ambulance from the corner. Me and Vernon. Rapunzel whispers again, not from caution but from shock. Who did it? Prince is crying now, not bothering to try keeping her quiet. I don't know, Zel. Honest to God. Whose knife was it, she persists. Someone took it . . . it was mine . . . lost it in all the mix-up and shouting and kicking. It is not difficult for her to look him in the eye what with the glare of street lights and the glowing London sky. Was it you?

Prince hisses. No. But it was my knife. What you gonna do? Prince has stopped talking and hunches up on the ground.

Why'd you call me, she says, why'd you call me by my real name. She can't get another word out of Prince.

You'll have to go to the police, she says after a while. Prince comes to again. Not fucking likely. I'm black, remember. I live in Battersea. Rapunzel suddenly realises that she is not wearing make-up and has not brushed her hair. She hangs her head a little. You can't run away for ever she whispers.

Who says I fucking can't. You run. All the time.

Rapunzel is ice-cold. She feels as if Prince has carved a hole in her head and is sitting there crowding her out. She wants to be back in the room she shares with Tilly – Silly Tilly as the kids on the fifth floor say. She wants to hide under the blankets. Most of all she wants to be sitting on the floor with the man and playing with his wooden animals. She wants to grow down until she can go to sleep on his lap. Some of her sense of shock reaches Prince.

Well, he says, people know you're not . . . that there's something funny . . . about you and Tilly and your mum.

She's a drunk and Tilly's a mongol, snaps Rapunzel.

Prince moves further away from her, far enough for the street light to catch his face through the trees. He looks awful. I got to find out if Eddy's okay he says. You could do that for me. Tomorrow. Bound to be in St George's.

You think the police won't notice me, asking questions? What about the others? Your precious posse. Prince sighs. Watching their own damn black skins most likely. If Eddy's okay . . . blood always looks a lot . . .

Rapunzel feels guilty about wanting to know more. She presses her own hand against her mouth. They hear a police siren close and Prince jumps. They do it all night round here, she says.

If Eddy's okay, I could, kind of disappear for a bit. If you've got some cash . . .

Rapunzel is suddenly so tired she could pass out on the grass. So bloody unfair. All they want is someone to panic on . . . to take responsibility. And money. Cash, she says. Makes a change from sex. I've got a gold chain. You could sell that.

Can I stop over? Just for the bed. Rapunzel realises that Prince, the proud guy who picks and chooses, is pleading. She makes the most of it.

Only got two rooms, me and Tilly in one.

Tilly won't notice, he says, his voice still down and pathetic. Rapunzel retorts sharply. She's not that daft. She knows I'm not a six-foot black guy with no hair. Prince sighs again. Rapunzel gives a little. Of course, maybe mum's still pissed out of her head. We might be able to move Tilly. A voice in her head warns, don't give him even that, don't ever give any man even an inch. She is surprised by it, turns the words over, doesn't hear Prince's reply. He's on his feet. Quick. Let's get going. As she stumbles dreamily over the grass and he lifts her over the railings she can hear their footsteps magnified on the street.

After she has moved the stolidly sleeping Tilly and checked that her mum is not dead she tries to fall asleep. Prince breathes more easily than seems right. Every time, just as she is about to go off she jerks upright in a panic. How can he bloody sleep and leave her to worry. What if mum finds them? What if . . . she lies down, cramped in Tilly's little bed. A few moments later she is up again. Why does she hate that gold chain? It's worth something. Why sell it for Prince? What if Prince got out of bed now and . . . she feels sick. Not just a weird name, Rapunzel, she is weird, a freak, her body doesn't belong to her, she has never felt desire.

Just before dawn she has fallen asleep, properly. Nothing much different about waking up. Heavy sounds from upstairs like they're playing catch with the baby or doing a cockroach massacre. Traffic panting and moaning round the one-way system. What's different is that Tilly isn't muttering and chatting like she always does in the morning. It's her best time, the time when she's really sweet, looks as if she's counting her fingers and toes and making up great big sums that will solve all the world's problems. Just the sound of Prince snoring. Rapunzel blinks a bit and looks at the other bed. One arm hangs limp out of the bed and his toes stick out. She feels like tucking him up again but then she's anxious and angry and jumps out of bed, checking that her pyjamas are buttoned, and shakes him. I got to get Tilly back soon she hisses. Mum won't sleep for ever.

Prince doesn't know where he is nor what has happened. The big guy, the lord of the posse, and he's all confused. Then he knows, and sits up holding his head.

Get out the bloody bed, Rapunzel says, get in the bathroom while I dress and move Tilly. He swings his legs out, keeping the sheet wrapped between his thighs. You know what, he says. You care more about that fucking mong than you care about me. Rapidly, not thinking, she swipes him round the face and he grabs her by the wrists and they are both on the bed. You dare ever talk about my sister like that, she spits at him, still keeping her voice down because she knows there are always listeners. He twists her arms until she is horizontal beside him. Sister, he says. For fuck's sake, she's your bloody child.

Prince is squeezing a cold flannel full of water over her face. It is like she is a hundred fathoms under the sea, her lungs filling with water. When she puts a hand up and rubs her eyes, Prince is sitting on the floor looking anxious. 'Bout time someone said something, he says, looking guilty. He gets up and pulls on his jeans and shirt. You get Tilly and I'll chip, he says.

You got to convince me I'm awake, says Rapunzel. Do something. Pull my hair. Make me cry. Go on. *Pull my hair.* She's shouting, pleading. She can see Prince's face, knows what's going on in his head, get me out of this, I don't want no responsibility, want to run. She sits up and grabs his shoulder. *Pull my hair.*

Prince looks like he is undergoing some kind of frightful test. Like he's almost through a twenty-six-mile marathon and can't make the finish. Like he's in front of a burning building and can't burst through the blazing door to rescue the inmates. Like he's a baby who's asked to grow up in twenty seconds flat. She thinks he'll lose the race.

Then he pulls her hair. Like a bell tolling. He pulls and pulls and the tears start and she screeches. You're awake, says Prince.

Both of them sit there in a state of shock. No words. It lasts a long time but Rapunzel breaks first. She gets off the bed and steps over him, dragging the sheet with her, and goes to dress herself in the bathroom. She comes back with Tilly in her arms. Tilly's black, she says to Prince. Tilly sits on the other bed playing cat's-cradle with her fingers, watching them both with her slanty, copper eyes. You're telling lies, says Rapunzel.

It's what they say, says Prince.

They say, they say, mocks Rapunzel. They say you killed Eddy in a fight, yeah?

Prince looks at her in surprise. He's forgotten. Or made it up in the first place.

Rapunzel is sick to death of everything. Should have left you outside last night, she says, wanting him to get out of her life. Eddy did get stabbed, says Prince, looking hurt. Shit, it was my knife, Zel. And I got a record.

Lucky you, says Rapunzel. She goes over to sit by Tilly. Bloody lucky you. There are tears coming down her face and wetting her tracksuit like she is pouring a kettle over her knees. Prince doesn't look like the lord of the posse any more. He's thinking about hitting her, she guesses, cover up the way he seems to have shrunk inside his skin, the way his mouth is turned down. Big strong guy she thinks. Blind as a bloody bat. Can't feel a thing for anyone except his own stupid self. Go find Rachel, she tells him. She'll help. If she's that fucking stupid. Rapunzel is studying Tilly's hand, which sits very small inside her own, she waits for the slap round the face, but all she feels is a puff of air as the door opens and shuts. He's gone.

Half an hour later she is pushing the buggy into King George's Park and Tilly is chewing the lump of hard bread they've brought for the ducks. She parks Tilly by the water and sits on the grass, her head drooping so that her hair falls forward and cuts off the world. She tries to think of a mean word for Prince. So many mean words for girls, all she can think of for him is bastard, and that reminds her of what he said about Tilly. Rapunzel turns her head from side to side so that the hair swings around her face, letting in flashes of sunlight. She goes faster until she is sick and dizzy, whirling her head, swirling her hair, black and red flashes in her eyes, her head filling with noise like waterfalls, the top of her head coming loose, everything splintering and bursting like a firework, and the sky full of pictures.

179

There's the man, the one who has crept in and out of her head without a name or a face, the one who made wooden toys and tucked her up. There he is, he's got yellow-brown hair and sad blue eyes and he looks quite old, but most of all he looks like her and she knows he is her dad and there's nothing bad about him at all and he can't be, what she's not been able to think of thinking, he can't be Tilly's father because he's white, so either her mum has been with someone or she has.

There's another face, only it is hard to see because she starts shaking like a tree in a blizzard when it comes at her out of the sky, but it pushes its way through and all she can see is eyes like snails creeping into her skull and eating her brain and her skin is going cold and she thinks she is screaming. The face grows hands and a body and thick legs which are grinding at her and there are knives shooting up inside her and she wants to die.

You all right, duck, says someone and she opens her eyes. There's Tilly still chewing the bread and there's a woman touching her arm. Only you was shouting out and then it looked like you fainted or something. Rapunzel pokes around in her throat till she finds her voice. Thanks, she says. Thanks. Must have dropped off, dreaming, you know. Okay then, says the woman, looks like she's glad to move off quickly.

Rapunzel snatches the bread from Tilly and gets the pushchair moving fast. She knows there's only one thing to do now and after that there'll maybe be time to think about it all, but for now she can't think. She gets back to the flat and finds orange juice and biscuits for Tilly, walking like she's a clockwork dog, wound up with a key, not responsible for where she goes. She's in her mum's room dragging her out of bed and dumping her on the sofa and sitting opposite waiting for the sleep to clear and the hungover buzz in her ears to die down. Then she's shouting. The words come scalding out like she's a water jet someone's unplugged.

All the lies, all the lies, Rapunzel screams. What did you do with my dad. You got rid of my dad. You tell me where my dad is, and I never had no pneumonia did I, liar, liar, I was having a baby wasn't I, I was raped wasn't I, you want me to think my dad did it don't you, my dad ain't black is he, I know my dad, Tilly's got a black dad, what did you make them do to my brain, I've been brain dead haven't I, what you want me for, then. Me and Tilly. You never do no damn thing for us, shut us up in this poxy flat, away from . . . away from . . . she stops because her anger is all mixed up in sorrow, and if she's been a water jet one minute now she's a frozen pillar of ice.

Her mum's not crying. She's got that look on her face like she's going to wriggle out somehow.

It's what they told me, her mother says, defiant, pulling her nightie down over her white sticks of leg. Too much more shock and you'd be in the nuthouse. Leave her think Tilly's mine. She is whining now, a beautiful whine she puts on beautifully, made myself a whore for you I did, making out I'd been with someone just to make you happy. I did what they said. You bring up Tilly like yours, they said.

Rapunzel melts back a little. No they didn't. No one'd tell you to be that cruel. It's him, isn't it, something about him. She leans forward and shakes her mother hard. Tell me about him.

Him! Her mother spits it out. Bastard. Left me and took you, didn't he. Told everyone things. Like I was a nutter. Not safe with you. Like I was a drunk and had men in. Her eyes swivel towards the gilt trolley where she keeps the gin. Rapunzel reaches out and turns her mother's head to face front. I got him though, her mother says, and starts laughing. I got him. Worth being dumped with you two it was, to see him like that. Pleading, crying he was. I want my child he said, she needs me he said. Like killing a cockroach it was, stamping on him, seeing him off. Hearing them all, can't trust a man to look after a kid. Dirty bugger. Good as put you on the game. Let that bastard mate of his in the house to mess with you. Had another think then, they did. A girl's all right with her mum, they said. See. Got a mum what's been set up, shit on.

Rapunzel sees her mother blowing up like a bubble, puffing her cheeks out, making up stories. Give me time, she thinks, I'll remember, I'll know it's all wicked stories. The man she remembers. The one who made her toy animals. He begins to come back, floating out of a mist, an uncertain shape at first, then the mist clearing. Her mother starts to roll about, laughing, hugging her goose-pimpled arms round her pouchy breasts. Rapunzel is no longer feeling sad. Her anger sharpens her memory and she knows that she can do it now.

Her voice is like the knife she wants to reach for. Give me his address. Her mother stops laughing and looks cunning. Rapunzel reaches for her throat. She can't help herself. Her fingers almost meet round the thin neck and she pushes with her thumbs, loving the way they sink between muscle. The address, she says, softly. Her mother scrabbles with her hands and Rapunzel's thumbs slacken. She lets her mother go, watches her totter over to the box of video tapes and take out a piece of lined paper. Rapunzel gets her a pen. She sits down again, sucking the pen.

And if you're lying, I'll come back and kill you, says Rapunzel, still very soft. Her mother writes. You're not allowed, she says, putting on her moany voice. You'll get into trouble. It's the law. Her voice gets stronger. She is still holding the paper. He's the one who's mad. He's bloody mad. They ought to have locked him up. Gave you some stupid name. Her eyes go distant. First row we had. Over your bloody name. Fairy-tale girl, he said. Bloody nonsense. I taught him though. I saw him off.

She begins to cackle and rock herself on the sofa. You brought the book home from school, she said. Rapunzel, Rapunzel, let down your golden hair! He went blind, the Prince did. Thorns in his eyes. She laughs and laughs. Never saw you again.

Rapunzel forgets about the knife. Her mother seems to grow very small, as if she is seeing her from the end of a street. She looks about ninety. Not worth killing. She'll die soon enough. One day she'll fall on the floor and throw up, no one to get the shopping, she won't eat, she'll just puke and choke. Rapunzel can see her, thin as a ghost, on the floor with her mouth open, sick mixed in her hair, cockroaches swarming on her eyes.

Rapunzel picks the paper from her hands. Fairy-tales are silly. Make out that what happens to you comes out of the blue like wind and rain and can just be washed out like tea stains. No one bothers about money, about how to get to Birmingham with Tilly and a pushchair and a suitcase. If he's there. If he wants her. She's not sure whether she wants him either but she needs to get the story straight. Then she'll decide, when she's real, solid, no longer someone's dream.

She goes up to Tilly and lets her hair swing round them both so that for a moment they are face to face in a golden bowl. Rapunzel kisses her funny blank eyes. Hello pet, she says.

Across the Line

Emily Perkins

SOMETIMES, WHEN SHE'S homesick, Megan remembers the pale, early winter day eleven months before when she'd boarded the large boat in her small harbour town. Her mother and father had stood safely ticketless on the dock and freedom was out there, just beyond the headland. Sometimes, when she's homesick, she can still feel the pressure of her parents' determinedly dry kisses on her cheeks and forehead. When she's homesick, she stands on the back doorstep of her flat, blinking tears at the pitiful English garden in the dull English light and hating even the air she is breathing because it's English air. But she hasn't had that bruised, trembly feeling for a long time, for at least two months. She's settled in here now. The Megan who stood on the dock, other, nineteen-year-old Megan, is very remote and far away. She was left behind at the bottom of the ship's swimming pool when they crossed the equator.

Who's a first-timer? the steward had shouted, his white shirt glaring in the white heat reflected from the deck. The men were held down in canvas deckchairs and instructed not to move a muscle as a crew member advanced on them wielding shaving soap and a razor. The girls and women were lined up by the pool, shrinking back, giggling, from the edge, jostling one another to the front. Megan found herself there, the weight of the group behind her, male hands suddenly gripping her ankles and wrists. Her legs lifted from the deck and she twisted her neck to see the purser laughing by her feet, the planed jaw of Mr Price, the Canadian bachelor, above her

187

face. His quiet, amused smile. They'd swung her, hammock-like, one, two, three, and she was released – flung – in a curve – a moment of gaping terror – her body flew through the air in one direction and the ship plowed through the water in the other, it was wrong, they were going to miss, she would fly over the edge into the ocean or tumble on to the deck below – the sickening crack of her breaking back – then she was plunged deep into the pool and felt her legs scrape gently on the bottom and she kicked and rose gasping through the sur-face skin of the water and out into the northern hemisphere, the other side of the world.

That night, New Megan had let Mr Price the Canadian bachelor place his hands on her hips and pull her awkwardly towards him. They were not, as she would have liked, leaning against the ship's railing with the moon suspended luminous above. They were in the corridor behind the galleys. The smell of peas and corned beef hung gluey in the air between them. New Megan had pretended to enjoy Mr Price's kisses. She had sighed and drooped and when he was finished she looked slowly – slowly – up at him from beneath her lashes. Truly, she'd wanted to enjoy it, to feel desire, even to be carried away – but she didn't know how. She was distracted by his scratchy cheek, by the frightening grown-up smell of sweat and by that same amused, detached expression in his eyes. The boat had pitched suddenly, or she imagined that it did, and she escaped down the corridor, up the slippy metal stairs, back to her cabin, the door locked tight behind her. Nothing was visible outside her porthole but the dark blue-black that could have been either sky or sea.

The next evening Mr Price asked Megan to marry him. This was her third marriage proposal. The first had been from Harry Cleary, the only boy she'd ever let touch her under her skirt. She'd turned him down and a year later he was in a motorcycle accident, somehow came off a country road one night and lay in a ditch with the bike on top of him until morning. He died on the way to the hospital. Houdini, they used to call him, because he could always get out of a tight corner. He was the first boy to propose to Megan and then he disappeared, vanished, melted into thin air for ever. The second proposal had been from Peter, the boy she was going out with before she left home. She hadn't even paused to consider that one. He was stuck there and she was gone already, in her mind. And then there was Mr Price, who she couldn't possibly marry because Megan Price had been the name of a fat unpopular girl at her school and besides, she suspected that he'd only asked her in order to persuade her into bed. Sometimes she suspected that of Harry and Peter as well, that they wanted to be engaged so that she'd sleep with them. And then perhaps they'd behave in such a way that she didn't want to marry them after all, and she'd have to break off the engagement, except she wouldn't be a virgin any more. It wasn't that she was a prude, but sleeping around was something a nice girl didn't do, and if Megan wasn't a nice girl she didn't know who or what she might be.

Her best friend Eithne's not a virgin.

– Of course, she'd said to Megan's poorly concealed shock.

– It's fun as long as you're careful. We're not Muslims for God's sake.

What shocks Megan the most is that Eithne discusses her boyfriends with her mother. Megan could never do that. She lies to her mother and father about nearly everything these days. Small lies, lies of omission, lies to stop them worrying – so many that she's lost count. The biggest lie is about her flat, which she shares with a girl and two boys. It's perfectly innocent but her mother would not believe that. She wouldn't understand that it's the modern thing to do.

Saturday morning. Megan's supposed to be doing her hand-washing – Jackie Kennedy recommends taking a set time each week to catch up on personal grooming maintenance – but the pale-orange sunlight shifting across the living-room has sent her into a warm daze. For some reason the irritating face of the mailroom boy at work keeps floating up on to the backs of her closed eyes. She squeezes them hard and shakes her head. He thinks he can pick on her, just because she's the newest and the youngest in the office. The first time she'd taken the letters down there, rushing because it was nearly five, and itchy in her new work dress and woollen tights, he'd looked up and leered in an unpleasant way. His ears stuck out.

Who's this then, he'd said, staring somewhere below her neck. She told him her name and to her annoyance bent her knees in a small deferential bob, just like the one she gave her female boss because she didn't know if it was right to shake her hand.

He snickered. – Megan, he said, rubbing his right-angled earlobe, – are you a virgin?

For a second she wasn't sure if she'd heard him right, but his loose wet mouth convinced her. She managed not to fling the letters at him and placed them carefully on the table, standing as straight as she could, her lips pressed hard together.

– I thought so, he called after her as she walked out the door. She couldn't help it, she stamped her foot, and another nasal laugh followed her up the stairwell. She hated him.

– Little toe-rag, Eithne had said, – I'd have given him what for. But she couldn't quite hide the laughter in her eyes. And now, stretching her feet out over the arm of the couch, Megan finds a smile widening on her face too.

– What are you doing?

She jerks up into a sitting position. Tea spills over the rug. She runs to the kitchen for a cloth and scrubs at it, batting her flatmates' legs out of the way.

– We're going into Chelsea. Want to come?

– No. Yes. Just a minute.

There's a wine and cheese party that night in St John's Wood, near streets with names like Blenheim and Marlborough. At home there are streets with those names too. A lot of things from home are echoed here. She'd thought of it that way round when she first arrived, until London solidified and became concrete under her feet and home became a shadow, like the watered-down imitation that it was. There, whole cities and towns were named after English ones. It was a joke how tiny and empty they were compared to the real thing. At home, winding behind the native forest on the outskirts of the town, there was a River Thames.

– Let's have this now, says Eithne, holding out a bottle of fizzy wine. She's come by to take Megan to the party. – Not black again. You're so *boring.*

– I like black. I was never allowed to wear it at home. Only to Uncle Ray's funeral and then it was one of mummy's frocks.

Balancing two glasses in one hand and the bottle and a cigarette in the other, she sashays from the kitchen back into the living-room. Eithne's crouched down beside the record player, flicking through Tom's collection. While she's not looking, Megan strikes a pose like out of a fashion magazine. Black is for fast women, it's elegant and secretive. She loves this dress with a strange passion she hasn't felt for anything since she tried on the long gloves for the school leavers' ball when she was eighteen.

Eithne turns and stands up. – Come on then. This is the latest dance. I'll teach you.

On Sunday, Megan has to visit her cousin who lives miles and miles away, virtually out of London. It takes an hour and a half on a tram and a bus. Norma isn't really her cousin but some obscure relation who has always lived in this remote part of London and never been further than France, let alone the other side of the world. Megan was instructed by her mother to see Norma at least once a month. After the visits Norma writes a detailed letter to Megan's parents, so she has to make sure and tell her the same lies as she tells them. Norma's husband Jack is a strange man from somewhere in the North who breeds hamsters for show purposes. They don't have any children. Today Jack is in the garden shed.

– He's training his vegetables.

– I beg your pardon?

Norma hands Megan a tepid cup of tea. – There's a pet and garden show next month. They give a prize for the most unusual shaped vegetable. Jack was runner-up last time and now he's determined to win it. He grows them in little pots and ties string around them to make them bend a certain way, then replants them. Potatoes are the most effective.

– Oh.

– You should come along. They have some wonderful sights. It's the twenty-fifth, we'll drive you. Once I saw a marrow this big.

– Thanks. That would be – nice.

– So, have you been having a marvellous time? Tell me all about the theatre last night.

After a while Norma takes a plate of shortbread out to the potting shed. Megan lets her head flop back against the arm-chair, exhausted. The life she describes to Norma and her parents is one of racing from museum to art gallery, West End show to botanic garden, public lecture to classical concert. The only music she's seen since arriving in London has been in sweaty dark pub basements, shaggy-haired boys with gui-tars and drums and swively hips. Her parents wouldn't under-stand that she likes to spend her time in cafés or shopping with Eithne or at parties like the one last night. They would say that she wasn't making the most of London, that she'd regret her missed opportunities when she was back home and starting her real life – married to a young man with a degree from the local university and raising children and being expert in the finer points of flower arranging. She won't be expected to travel again, not like this, being independent. What Megan sometimes thinks is that she might not go home at all, that she might stay here where she is free, where it's enough like home to be comfortable but not so much like home that she wants to leave it.

The party had been brilliant. It was jammed full with all sorts of people who were dancing and joking, drinking out of bottles and each others' glasses, smoking cigarettes and shak-ing their heads to the music in the new way. She slouches fur-ther down in Norma's armchair and closes her eyes. Eithne had kissed a ginger-haired man in the hallway and later a fel-low with glasses on had tried to kiss Megan but she ducked away, laughing. She'd danced and danced and someone had pushed open the aluminium-framed window to let in fresh air and when she was burning up from dancing she'd leaned out of it, breathed deeply, beamed up at the viscous brown city sky. Neighbours came round to complain about the noise – the room began to empty – she got a lift back with some nice peo-ple, a married couple and another boy. The noise of the party is in the room with her now, the close heat of bodies moving

against each other, the smell of cigarettes and wine and some jonquils that had been sitting in a milk bottle by the window –
 – Megan?
She opens her eyes and yawns straight into Norma's hamsterish face. – Oh. Sorry.
 – You must have been knocked out by that play. It is strenuous watching live performance. I haven't been in years, mind you.
Megan smiles and takes a sip of her stone-cold tea and wonders if Norma isn't fooled for one minute by all her elaborate routines.
Later, as Megan's about to leave, Norma asks the inevitable question. – And what news of your brother?
Richard lives in France. He's been there two years and is married to a mean-lipped Frenchwoman called Sylvie. Megan had stayed with them over New Year. Sylvie spent the whole time moaning in French and jiggling their new baby in a fractious way. She was very beautiful despite the mouth, from an intellectual family, and Megan couldn't understand why she'd married Richard until she did some maths concerning the date of the wedding and the baby's age. They never wrote to each other, she and Richard, and she hasn't seen him since January, but – He's very well I think, is what she says now.
 – And the baby? Is he crawling yet? Norma's face twitches and Megan has to look away. Norma and Jack are the only older couple she knows without children. She'd love to ask why they never had a family but doesn't know how. It would be unbearable if she made Norma cry. She tries to check the time on her watch without being noticed.

Next weekend, after it's stopped raining, she and Eithne go for a long walk in Regent's Park. Eithne tells her all about the date she went on the night before with the red-haired bloke from the party.
 – He was gruesome. I opened the front door and he was standing there with a rose between his teeth.
 – He never.
 – He bloody did. Didn't stop his breath from stinking, either.

– Did you kiss him again?

– I had to. He took me to a nice restaurant. She makes a face at the memory.

– Did you ask him in?

– Get off. He thought he was so smooth. Wish I'd stayed home. What did you do?

– Stayed home. Did some handwashing.

– Not your Jackie Kennedy evenings again. Did you brush your hair a hundred times as well? She pulls Megan's cap off and ruffles her hair. – Oh, so clean and shiny.

Megan jumps for her cap but Eithne backs away, waving it like a trophy.

– Come here. Give it back. You bugger.

– Megan. I don't think Mrs Kennedy would use that sort of language now, would she?

– Give it back. She lunges after it and falls against Eithne, who pushes her off and dances out of range.

– What did you call me?

– I called you a bugger. A bloody bloody bugger.

They chase each other down the slippery wet path. Suddenly Eithne skids to a stop.

Megan snatches the cap out of her hands. – What?

– I thought I heard someone say your name.

They stand still for a second, trying to listen above the sound of their panting breath. Only dogs and distant traffic. Megan pulls her hat down tight over her ears and link arms with Eithne. – Shall we go to the caff? Do you feel guilty not being in church? I don't.

– Megan! It's a man's voice and all of a sudden he's there, breathing heavily from running, bending forward, hands on his knees, grinning up at her with crooked teeth. Megan and Eithne took at each other, then back at him. – Hi, he says. – I was shouting. Don't know if you heard me.

– No, says Megan. – Hi.

– Hi, he says again.

– Hello, says Eithne.

– Hi.

He straightens up. – Are you just starting a walk, or just fin-ishing one? I've been walking for ages. Get out of the house.

Fancy coming to the pub?

Megan looks over his shoulder at Eithne's crinkled eye-brows. – We were just going to have a cup of tea.

– Oh all right then. Mind if I join you? He turns to Eithne and holds out his right hand. – I'm David. If that's all right? He turns back to Megan. – If I won't be in the way?

– No, of course not. Yes I mean, that's fine. This is Eithne.

– I think we've danced together already. There's a nice tea-shop over this way. Well, you'd know, wouldn't you, he smiles at Megan. – We dropped you off somewhere around here.

– How much did you have to drink at that party? asks Eithne when they're back at Megan's flat making toast.

– I didn't think it was that much. But I couldn't remember him at all.

– Me neither. Was it his car?

– I don't know. I thought it belonged to the couple, but maybe he was driving. She frowns, then remembers not to. Don't want to get wrinkles. – I thought the single boy in the car had blond hair, but that can't be right. Otherwise David'd be one of the couple, and no. That can't be right.

– A boyfriend with a car. Brilliant. I'm fed up with motor-bikes, my hair gets ruined.

– Do you think he was nice?

– He thought you were.

– No. Really?

– Oh, come on. Is there any marmalade? Bet you he phones.

And he does, three days later, from a telephone box.

– It's stupid I know, but I've just shifted flat and the phone's not connected yet. How are you? It's so unusual to just bump into someone like that. I really enjoyed it.

– I don't think it's happened to me before, not in London.

He laughs. – It's fate then. Do you want to meet again this weekend? Saturday, in the park? We could go to an afternoon movie if it's raining.

– I . . . She was supposed to go to a football game with Eithne. – Yes, all right.

– Two o'clock then. In the same place, by the statue.

195

She's five minutes late, and nervous, but he isn't there yet. This is her first English date – the group outings and mixed parties don't exactly count. She wishes it wasn't sluttish to smoke in public. Perhaps he won't show up at all. It would be humiliating but a relief as well. She barely knows him. If she closed her eyes right now, she wouldn't be able to imagine his face. She wraps her arms around herself and tries it. Straight eyebrows; a long nose; those teeth; no, she can't. There's a tap on her arm and she opens her eyes.

– You didn't know who I was when I saw you last week, did you?

They're in the tea-shop, at the same table by the corner. Eithne's seat is empty but Megan still feels her presence, watching drily from the other side of the table.

– Well no. I didn't. Sorry.

He laughs with his crooked teeth. – No need to apologise. Some days I have difficulty remembering myself.

– It's not that I was drunk—

– I know. You were tired. And very sweet. It was a good party. I don't like parties as a rule. I like that flat though. Nice and modern. What's yours like?

He talks so much there's barely time to notice all the things he says. He'll slip something into the conversation and keep going without waiting for her response. He seems very open for someone who's lived in London all his life. Well, he's trav-elled all over the Continent, too. Spent a year in Italy. That's what made him decide to be an architect. The ancient Romans built tenement blocks, did she know that? Functional as well as beautiful. Clean lines. Italians are so wonderfully frank and passionate – but still, he says, there was something strange he missed about England, the repression, he knows it's not a fashionable opinion but it makes life more interesting, don't you think? More secretive, more mysterious?

No one's ever spoken to Megan like this before in her life. She gulps her tea and scalds the top of her tongue.

– Tell me about where you're from, he says, lighting a ciga-rette and looking at her from a three-quarter profile. – I want to know all about it. I've never travelled that far. Do you know where I'd really love to go? Malaya. I have an uncle there with a sugar plantation. It would be brilliant to go out and see how they live – bamboo huts I suppose – can you imagine. Travel is the most wonderful thing. It broadens the mind. It was my political awakening, travelling through Europe. The workers, the peasants – their lives are terribly harsh, terribly beautiful. Have you found that the big city's opened your mind? I hear your country is totally unspoiled. Did you appreciate that while you were there?

– No, not really—

– I didn't appreciate the comforts of English life until I'd hitchhiked across France and Spain. Different approaches to hygiene. And manners. And driving. But such committed, politicised people. Christ, I'm rambling. I must be nervous, he suddenly mumbles, and then smiles at her. – I'm really just a romantic.

Megan is shocked. A boy from home would die before admitting to a thing like that. Romance wasn't to be discussed, it was a hazy, cloudy thing that women demanded and men had to reluctantly supply. Her mother and father had never once displayed affection towards one another – not in her presence at least. Harry Houdini had been charming, but in a mischievous, schoolboy way. Even when he'd asked her to marry him she hadn't been sure if he was serious or not. And Peter and her brother and all the other boys she knew – they were shiny-nosed lunks, they handed over bunches of limp carnations on Valentine's Day with all the enthusiasm of a child holding out its hand to be smacked. And here was David describing himself as a romantic. She doesn't know what to say.

– I suppose you've got a lovesick youth waiting for you back home, have you? She stares at him. – No, never mind, he grins, – there are some topics we'd better not go into, yeah? You agree?

She nods her head in a robotic way.

– Great. We've got a deal then. Listen, can I call you next week? We could meet up, maybe go to the cinema? I'd like to see you again. Maybe, he says, almost inaudible as he reaches round the chair for his jacket, – we could go to a nightclub.

He pays for the tea and walks her to the end of the road, where he kisses her on both cheeks and gives her shoulders a brief squeeze before breaking into a run, waving wildly as he vanishes around the corner.

– We're going out tonight. Rusty's got a friend.

– You said he was awful.

– He is. But they've got tickets to the Royal Court. So. Are you in love?

– Don't be silly.

– Are you going to see him again?

– He said he'd call. Megan pulls the phone line round as far as it will go into the kitchen corner. She peers at her flatmates, engrossed in a television show. – Eith, you've got to tell me. She grits her teeth then says as quickly as possible: – How do you do it?

– Do it?

– You know. It.

– You know what happens, don't you? You must.

– Yes I do know but – so you're good?

– Jesus Christ. Poor David. Does he know what he's in for?

– Don't worry. Let's not talk about it.

– Look. It's just—

– I—

– It's different for everyone, I suppose. You've just got to see what happens.

– Fine. Thanks. Sorry.

– Are you serious about this bloke though? You've only met him twice.

– Eithne—

– Mm?

– Do you think I'm square?

– No. You're nice and curvy. Now shut up.

In the tea-shop next Saturday, she feels foolish for even having thought of sleeping with him. He's friendly enough, but seems distracted and doesn't mention the possibility of seeing a movie or going dancing. She's cross with herself for having kept the evening free.

– I'm sorry, I've got to go, he says at last. – Bad timing. I'm giving a talk at my CND group tonight.

– Isn't that a communist party organisation?

– No, he says, snapping alight a match. – That's a common myth. Some of our members have certain political affiliations, of course, but we're an anti-nuclear campaigning group. That's all. He looks at her, then reaches out and strokes his finger along her eyebrow. – You should come along one evening. Not tonight, but another time. God, I've got to run. Same time next week?

Dear Mummy and Daddy, thinks Megan, the tingle in her eyebrow travelling sweetly all through her body, *I'm going to have sex with a revolutionary. I'm never coming home.*

– We're going for a drive. Her three flatmates are squeezed in the doorway of Megan's bedroom. – Want to come?

– No thanks. She smiles in their general direction, eyes unfocused to avoid contact. – Bye.

As the door closes, she brings her thumb up to her mouth in an unthinking way and starts to suck. Her other hand draws the blankets up under her chin. The letter with her brother's handwriting on it falls to the floor. No one in her family has ever got a divorce. No one in their family ever raised their voices to anyone. No one in their family uses words like failure, and heartache, and bitterness. He doesn't know what will happen to the baby. His ticket home brings him through London in six week's time. Megan slides under the bedclothes until they cover her head. She's cold.

They don't ever go further than the tea-shop or the park together, but as late spring progresses into early summer Megan feels that progress is definitely being made. She sees their meetings as part of a love story, and it doesn't occur to her to question this. Everything she's ever learned about male and female relationships leads her to assume that this is the beginning of something for them. The middle is slightly blurred – it involves him taking her to bed – but the end of the story is in perfect focus, set in a register office with David looking dishy in a new suit and Eithne standing proudly by her side. And it is true that they become more familiar to one another. She learns to anticipate the way he pinches the bridge of his nose and folds his arms when he's laughing. She knows that he will wait until the first pot of tea is empty before lighting a cigarette. She becomes used to listening to him talk – about travel, a house he's designing, the threats of pollution and nuclear bombs. Nothing about his life, though, beyond work and the CND. Nothing personal.

 She tells him about the bands she's seen on Friday night or what's happened in the office that week. One day he's unusually quiet and she starts talking about home, about the farm they used to stay on in the Christmas holidays, washing dishes in the river and the swimming hole so deep no one could ever touch the bottom, not even Richard who was a champion diver at his school. She tells him about the mountains and how you could walk for hours along the long flat road leading towards them but they never came any closer. She remembers the magpies, and the cold barky smell of mud, and the hard shine of stars when black night sank down.

 – It's lonely sometimes, living in a place where everybody knows you. The endless brick of London, she borrows a phrase of his without being aware of it – I don't know, it's comforting in a way. She picks a piece of fluff off her cardigan. – My brother's going back.

He taps his ash, inhales and looks at her. – With his wife?

 – No, she says and her voice comes out hoarse. – On his own. She tries to smile in a carefree, worldly way but it crumbles on her face and her eyes fill with tears. She tips her head back and blinks fast. When she looks back to him he is frowning.

 – Promise me something, he says, taking a last draw from his cigarette and stumping it out.

 – What?

He leans forward in his chair, over to her side of the table. – Don't ever get married.

Her eyes widen. A tear drops quickly on to her cheek.

That was the day they kissed. When they left the tea-shop the wind had sharpened. The way he put his arm around her was protective at first. As they crossed the street to the sun-lit side they pressed closer, warmer together. David stopped walking. He held her lightly under the elbows, right there in the middle of the path.

– I've never seen a girl so distracted, says Eithne over her shoulder to Megan as they queue for cinema tickets, – it's disgusting. Rusty hasn't called you know. Toe-rag.

After the movie they go for coffee and a fag in the café next to the theatre. – God, that was brilliant. Eithne shovels sugar into her coffee and stirs it lazily, scraping the spoon around the bottom of the mug. – Do you think I'd look good with my hair like her, the main one?

– Pardon?

Eithne sighs. – Where is loverboy then, picketing Aldermaston?

– No. Megan tidies her skirt over her knees. – I don't know what he's doing today.

– Well I want to meet him again, could you tell him that? Ask him round for a drink.

– Don't you think I ought to wait for him to ask me?

– In an ideal world, yes.

– He told me he was a romantic.

– An incredibly slow one.

– I wish— Megan slumps back in her chair and lets her head bang against the wall. – I want—

– Yeah we know what you want. Eithne laughs. – I just hope he gets smart enough to figure it out.

So next weekend when David holds the tea-shop door open for her, she doesn't step inside. She stands looking up at him, her back to the cool, dark interior and smell of icing sugar, yeast and dripping.

– Do you want to come up to my flat, she asks, forcing herself to hold his gaze. – For coffee?

He isn't the sort of person who wanders around a new house picking objects up and turning them over absentmindedly. Nor does he study each photograph on the chest of drawers in her bedroom. He only glances around as if he's thinking of something else, then sinks into the large living-room armchair.

201

In the kitchen, Megan makes Nescafé and arranges malt biscuits on to a plate, conscious of the silence between the rooms.
– There's magazines in the rack, she calls out, but when she carries the tray through he's just staring straight ahead, smaller than usual in the enormous chair.

– Typical conversion this, he says as if he's talking to himself. – Should lower the ceiling and put a modern window in. He flicks his eyes up to the cornice. – Get rid of this Victorian rubbish.

She places a cup of coffee on the floor by his foot and backs away to perch on the sofa against the opposite wall. Through the offending sash window she can see the wall of the house across the street. It's glowing with yellow afternoon light. A mushroom-coloured cloud hangs over the roof. When she looks back to him he has closed his eyes. A flash of anger crosses her stomach. Then, – Megan?

– Yes?

– Are you scared?

She almost laughs. – Yes.

His eyes are still shut. – I am too. He pats the arm of the chair. – Come here.

Later, she asks if he wants to go into the bedroom.

– No, he says, stroking under her chin. – Not today. Shall I come back next week? Will your flatmates be out?

– I think so. She's unable to stop herself from smiling. – Yes, come back then.

– I'll phone you. I promise.

And he does. He calls her on Monday, Tuesday and Wednesday in her lunch-break at work. They chat about anything, ridiculous things, the weather and what he's seen walking to the tube that morning and the way her boss has of coming back from the ladies' with fresh lipstick smeared across her teeth. There's a new lightness between them, an ease made alive with anticipation. Megan takes her job less seriously. She jokes with the jug-eared mailroom boy, even enjoys his clammy stare. She doesn't tell Eithne about what's happening. She feels selfish, and possessive in a way she hasn't known before. This is hers and David's, she thinks, nothing to do with girliness. She senses a shift in herself, feels herself becoming different.

When the telephone on her desk shudders and rings at noon on Thursday she pauses to admire its sleek square blackness before picking up the receiver. – She's wearing white lips today, she says, – so you can't tell it's all over her teeth.

– Hello? Could I speak to Megan please?

– Hello?

– Is Megan there please?

– Norma. It's me. I'm sorry, I was talking to one of the other girls here.

– Oh I see. Lucky I'm not anyone important then!

Sometimes Norma can sound remarkably like Megan's mother.

– How are you? Megan asks, feeling the usual guilt at not having called. – Are you well?

– Yes, everything's the same here. I had a lovely letter from your mother last week. She said they hadn't heard from you in some time.

– Oh. Megan hopes David isn't trying to ring through.

– I said I was sure you'd written. The post can be so unreliable these days.

– Yes, I have, well—

– And how's your lover?

– I'm sorry?

– Richard, any news of him?

– Oh my brother. Ah. He's well I think. Has mummy heard from him?

– No neither of you. She's quite worried about her two babies.

– We're fine, really.

– Good. Now, I'm telephoning about this Saturday.

How could she possibly know? – Saturday?

– Yes, we've got you a ticket.

– Oh the show. Oh. Ah. Oh gosh. Um.

Silence from the other end.

– Oh dear, I think – what time is it?

– The show's all afternoon. I thought we'd collect you in the car, have a spot of lunch first, there's a nice pub nearby.

– Norma, I'm so sorry. I've completely double-booked myself. My friend Eithne's got tickets to the ballet, the Russian ballet, Margot Fonteyn, well I'm not sure it will be her, but that company, oh how stupid of me not to realise it was the same day.

– Are the Russian ballet in London? There hasn't been much publicity.

– Yes it's just a short tour, only two nights and Friday, the other night, was sold out.

More silence.

– Do you think – could you possibly find someone else to take my ticket for the show? Or I could give you the money for it.

– No don't be silly. Well, that is a shame. Jack and I were looking forward to seeing you.

– I'm really sorry.

– Well it can't be helped. Do give us a call when you've a spare minute, won't you.

– Of course. Norma, I—

– Bye then.

Megan stares at the telephone for the next twenty minutes, not leaving to buy a sandwich in case it rings.

Saturday. The morning. She runs a bath and sits on the edge, watching the water rise in the tub, overcome with a sense of inertia. The house is empty, silent except for the running water. Megan pulls off her candlewick dressing-gown, unbuttons the front of her nightie and draws it off over her head. Eyes closed against her naked body, she lowers herself into the hot bath. She washes herself in a dispassionate way, pushing aside the thought that she is preparing a sacrifice. It's three days since he last phoned.

Clean and perfumed in her black dress, she flicks through yesterday's paper. Rehashed stories about call-girls and government secrets. A threat to the security of British society. She opens the living-room window. Looks at the paper again. Lights a cigarette. There's a knock at the door.

They sit side by side on the sofa, sipping wine that he's brought and moving a bit to the music. The record ends. She stands up to change it and he takes her hand. She turns to look at him, still sitting there, smiling with his crooked mouth. He pulls her back down to him.

In her room later he says, – Shall we take a bath?

– I don't think there's any hot left.

– Oh. Megan. He shifts his arm out from under her. – I have to go.

She hasn't thought as far as him leaving.

– Will you be all right?

– Yes.

– You promise me?

– Yes.

– You're lovely.

It's not, I love you. All the same, she smiles. – Is your phone on yet?

He reaches for his trousers. – No. The truth is, I can't afford it right now. But I'll call you. Tomorrow. There's a meeting, CND, but I'll phone after that. He leans over and kisses her neck, then touches where he's kissed. – You're lovely, he says again. – I don't want to leave you.

Then he does.

Is she different now? She thinks so. She feels – oh, a million things. Warm and happy. Desired, relieved. Frightened. Lost. She plays the afternoon back again and again in her mind, her mood lifting and sinking like a paper boat half-over, half-underneath the waves.

There are four phone calls on Sunday. The first is Eithne, asking if she wants to come to the theatre with her and Rusty.

– No thanks. I might be seeing David.

– Going well then. Let's speak soon, it's ages since I've seen you.

The next three calls are for her flatmates. Megan spends the evening trying to concentrate on the moving black and white of the television.

The days are achingly slow. They have been since she met David, with the waiting for their weekly meetings. Now they drag interminably, long summer days full of short dresses and shirtsleeves and bodies lazing in the hazy green park. The blades of the fan on Megan's desk turn slowly. She walks down to the river at lunch-time and sits watching it not moving. A

stranded fish wrapped tight around its lamp-post gapes silently at her. Grit collects on the back of her neck. You're lovely.
Sweat crawls down the sides of her arms. She wonders if she
might have done it wrong. There's piece about a CND protest
on the news. The faces in the background and under the ban-
ner are too fuzzy to identify. On Thursday evening she walks
to the offices of the Architecture Association and stands outside the door. A woman in a headscarf comes out carrying a
bucket and a mop. Megan wanders home.

Richard's train arrives on Friday night. She meets him at the
station, a thin figure in a summer macintosh holding one small
striped suitcase. They hug tightly.
– What about all your things?
– I've left them there. It's not – I don't want them.
– Oh Richard.
– Don't.
She's too scared to ask about the baby. She doesn't know
what to say to him. They link arms and he starts walking away
from the station, fast so she has to half-run to keep up.
– Is there a place we can eat near here? I'm starving.
– We're meeting Eithne at a restaurant by my flat. Is Italian
all right?
He turns a brief smile in her direction. – Anything but
French.

While he's in the men's they chat about nothing for a couple
of minutes until Eithne leans over the red tablecloth, thrusting
her face towards Megan. – What's been happening? Your flat-
mates are worried about you. I'm worried about you. Is it
David?
Megan screws up her nose. – I'll be fine.
– What's he done? Did you—
– Hello, Megan smiles up at her brother.
– Listen, how's cousin Norma? he asks, squeezing back into
the booth.
– Don't ask. We might have to visit them tomorrow night.
– Saturday night? says Eithne through a mouthful of
spaghetti. – Bollocks. You're coming to a party with me.

– I really don't think I'm—

– Shut up. You know the people, we went the other week. You both just need a good dance.

Despite herself, Megan's half-hoping that David will call that day. He could have lost her phone number, or be ill, or even called away on business – anything might have happened. When she and Richard go to the market she takes him on the route through the park, just keeping an eye out. In the tea-shop she sits facing the door, her gaze flicking up to each new face every time the doorbell pings. Eventually she resigns herself to going to the party. Eithne comes over and they have a few drinks first, get into the mood. By the time they leave the house Megan's making an effort not to let her stiletto heels twist underneath her.

As they climb the narrow stairs to the party, a palpable wave of noise and body heat blasts from the open door. Megan feels a finger poking her ribs. – Come on, Eithne says, – I can hear the music.

Inside, the crush is intense. The bookshelves are shuddering. Cigarette smoke hangs thickly from head height up to the ceiling, and there's a darker, sweeter smell that Megan supposes must be hash. Eithne pushes against her waist from behind. – Get rid of your handbag. Let's dance.

Megan looks round but Richard has already vanished into the crowd. She lets Eithne lead her to the centre of the living-room, where arms are moving up and down, heads are nodding and hips are turning to the rhythm of the Rolling Stones. The song ends and there's a pause. In that pause Megan turns to face the door. At that moment David walks through it. He looks at her. She looks at the woman close behind him. Long blonde hair, a black polo-neck. – Catherine, she hears somebody say in a rising voice, – and your commie husband. We're not too bourgeois for you then—

Through the window and above the talk there's the high cry of a seagull. The floor shifts underneath her, like the lurching of a boat. The music starts again.

Much, much later, in thirty years' time, Megan will be asked by her niece (another Megan, from Richard's second marriage to a freckle-faced, tennis-playing girl from home) what she was like in those early London years. She will blink, surprised, in the way she has that looks slightly batty since the bifocals. – Well, she'll say, stroking the crease at the side of her mouth, – I was basically – unformed, I suppose. She doesn't feel that now, this hot summer evening in 1963, the sounds and smells of the city in the busy room with her, David disappearing behind the dancing strangers. Now, if you were to tap Megan on the shoulder and tell her that in five years she'll have had four more lovers, that in ten she'll have two sons and have stopped counting lovers, that she'll move home and away again, that she'll live in a tent and wash her clothes by a stream and plant tomatoes naked, that she'll sleep with a woman and wonder if it's at last true love, that she'll run a successful business and care for a sick parent and that each of these phases will seem not part of a continuum but separate incarnations, individual lives, she would not believe you. She would not believe that in eighteen months' time she'll think of David without her throat hardening and sweat covering her palms. Or that after a few years she won't think of him at all. That he'll only appear again as an occasional figure in dreams: shadowy, amorphous, with one fanged tooth and a duplicitous smile. Now, in the densely beating room, she reaches out to steady herself on Eithne's arm, remembers to breathe, waits for the wave of seasickness to pass.

Biographical Notes

Nicola Barker was born in 1966 and lives in Hackney. She is the author of two collections of stories, *Love Your Enemies* (winner of the David Higham Prize for Fiction and joint winner of the Macmillan Silver Pen Award for Fiction) and *Heading Inland* (winner of the John Llewelyn Rhys Prize in 1997), as well as two novels, *Reversed Forecast* and *Small Holdings*. Her third novel, *Wide Open*, will be published by Faber and Faber in 1998. She is recognised as one of the most original writers of her generation.

Louis de Bernières is the author of four novels: *The War of Don Emmanuel's Nether Parts*, *Señor Vivo and the Coco Lord*, *The Troublesome Offspring of Cardinal Guzman* and *Captain Corelli's Mandolin*, which won the Commonwealth Writers' Prize, Best Book, 1995. In 1993 he was selected as one of the twenty Best of Young British Novelists. He lives in south London.

Doina Cornell was born in Cornwall in 1967, and when only a few months old was taken by her English mother back to Romania to meet her father, who had to wait two more years for permission to leave the country. Most of her childhood was spent on a six-year family circumnavigation of the world by yacht.

Damian Croft, born in 1966, studied musical composition at Dartington and has spent much time in Turkey, which has given him material for his writing.

Andrew Dempster worked in Australia for eight years in electronic engineering and holds a world-wide patent for a satellite navigation receiver. In 1992 he came to England to study for a PhD at Cambridge University. He has published widely in his area of expertise but 'Biting the Cord' is his first published piece of fiction.

Sheena Joughin was a textile designer for ten years and has been writing fiction for five. She is a previous winner of the short story competition organised by the London Arts Board and has had stories published in other anthologies. 'Lunchtime' forms an episode in a longer piece of fiction on which she is working.

Elizabeth Kay has won prizes for her short stories and has had twenty published in various magazines and anthologies. She has also written five radio plays for Radio 4. She works as a teacher and illustrator.

Reuben Lane was born in Ipswich in 1966. He works as a cinema usher when not writing. He has had a story published in another anthology: *Random Factor* (published by Pulp Faction).

Shaun Levin was born in South Africa in 1963. His stories have appeared in other anthologies and magazines. He teaches creative writing in London.

Emily Perkins was born in New Zealand in 1970 and attended the New Zealand Drama School in the late 1980s. She has lived in London since 1994, and her first collection of stories, *Not Her Real Name*, won the Geoffrey Faber Memorial Prize in 1997. Her first novel, *Leave Before You Go*, will be published by Picador in 1998.

Dorothy Reinders has been a teacher, a marimbist and a greengrocer, among other occupations. Survivor of many years in other places, she has found a home in Hackney.

Daphne Rock has published a collection of poetry, *Waiting for Trumpets* (Peterloo, 1997). She has worked as a teacher and a social worker. Her current occupations are: part-time work on complaints from young people in care; writing a novel; preparing a second poetry collection; being a grandmother; and a new-found passion for geology.

Jane Shilling is a journalist and mother. She lives in Greenwich.